Constable
Beneath the Trees

Constable
Beneath the Trees

NICHOLAS RHEA

ROBERT HALE · LONDON

ISBN 0 7090 5327 4

Robert Hale Limited
Clerkenwell House
Clerkenwell Green
London EC1R 0HT

Photoset in North Wales by
Derek Doyle & Associates, Mold, Clwyd.
Printed in Great Britain by
St Edmundsbury Press Ltd, Bury St Edmunds, Suffolk.
Bound by WBC Ltd, Bridgend, Mid-Glamorgan.

Contents

1   Seek and Ye Shall Find

There is pleasure in the pathless woods.
Lord Byron (1788–1824)

'Times are changing, Rhea.'

Sergeant Blaketon was pensive as he sipped a mug of coffee in Ashfordly police station. We were sipping together in the spacious enquiry office. On that Monday morning, things were comparatively peaceful and he had cleared his desk before 9.30. There had been no reported crimes overnight and no fresh problems to exercise his mind. Now that his in-tray was empty and his telephone quiet, he found time to suggest that I made the coffee – which I did. Thus he joined me for a chat. I had just returned after a fortnight's leave and had driven from Aidensfield to Ashfordly to collect my mail. Ashfordly was peaceful that morning – but so was Aidensfield. As I'd had no telephone calls before nine o'clock, I had left my hill-top police house for the short drive to Ashfordly.

'Times changing, Sergeant?' I asked. 'In what way?'

'Every way, Rhea,' he sipped from his mug. 'There's going to be new procedures, new technology, new forms to be filled in, new telephone systems, changes to beat boundaries, changes to the names of things, changes in the way we do our job ... did you know that the think-tank at Headquarters is considering the abolition of the policewomen's department?'

'No, I had no idea,' I had to admit. 'I've been away for a couple of weeks.'

'The pace of change is hotting up, Rhea. You've had two weeks away and in that time the whole concept of policing has altered. With my responsibilities, I can't go away, Rhea; I might return to find somebody else sitting at my desk. Do you realise that policewomen won't be specialists any more? They'll have to compete for promotion with the rest of us, Rhea, they'll patrol with the men, working nights, dealing with fights. Can you imagine working for a woman inspector, Rhea?'

'I've never really thought about it, Sergeant,' I had to admit. 'I would think that if a woman knew her job well enough, there'd be no problems ...'

'You youngsters are all alike, Rhea, you've no respect for the past, for well tried and tested procedures and structures. I can't see a woman constable sorting out a fight between a bunch of drunken yobbos. If a woman is patrolling the streets at night, the male officers will spend their time worrying whether she can cope and they'll be caring for her, not the public – and don't think your cushy rustic beat at Aidensfield will escape the eagle eyes of those at the top either!'

'They're not going to close me down, are they, Sergeant?'

'Now that you've been issued with radio-equipped minivans instead of motor bikes for your patrolling, Rhea, the powers-that-be believe that beats should be larger. There's going to be amalgamations, Rhea, amalgamations of rural beats.'

'Is there?' This was news to me.

'Bigger beats will be the rule, Rhea. If a rural constable from say, Pattington, decides to retire or is promoted, then the vacancy that occurs when he leaves might not be filled. That means his patch will disappear – it will be divided between the adjoining rural beats and the police house will be sold. That's just an example, Rhea, but that sort of thing is going to happen, mark my words. Bigger areas covered by fewer constables, that's going to be the trend.'

'Are you saying that Aidensfield rural beat might be closed down, Sergeant?'

'When you move on, Rhea, that would be a possibility, a very distinct possibility. I can't deny it. And as rural beats become larger, village constables will be expected to work in towns too. They'll do shift work, Rhea, part of which will be in the town and part of which will be on their own patch.'

'Town duties, Sergeant.' The notion was horrifying.

'If rural beats are amalgamated,' he had clearly been giving the matter some consideration or had read some documents relating to the subject, 'if rural beats are amalgamated, several constables in vehicles will patrol the area between them, working shifts. Eight-hour shifts. That would replace the present twenty-four-hour responsibility of constables like you. It would give you more time off, Rhea. Not a bad thing, perhaps?'

'But we rural bobbies need to work our own beats, Sergeant,' I said. 'We need to know all the people on the patch if we're to keep crime down. And the idea is that we live and work on the patch for twenty-four hours a day. I don't object to that, it's the best way of giving value for money, you work when the work's there and relax when it isn't.'

'That's not considered the way to do things in the new style of thinking, Rhea. Bigger beats shared between several constables is the new concept – and that's a new word in police jargon! Concept! And if you're on duty when someone else is patrolling your normal patch, you'll be drafted into town for additional urban patrols!'

'I don't think it's good idea.' I could see that if this scheme was adopted, the rural areas would be deserted by patrolling constables. In the minds of supervisory officers, towns were always short of constables and they would always be supplemented by rural officers. The demands of town-policing would always take priority.

Blaketon went on, 'You'll be working more hours in Ashfordly, Eltering and Strensford, Rhea, supplementing the officers in those busier places. Being motorized means you can cover a bigger area in the time available and being equipped with radio means you'll be in contact with Control all the time. You must admit there isn't much crime in Aidensfield, Rhea, there's no real need for a police presence there.'

'But if the village constable is removed from Aidensfield, Sergeant, crime will break out the minute he's gone! And there'll be no one around to deal with it, or report it to. It'll start with the kids vandalizing things, then they'll rise to petty thefts and even break-ins ... remove the constable from the streets and crime will increase, Sergeant. With no one in authority to prevent them, the kids will do as they like, and once they do as they like, they'll start to do wrong.'

'I know that, you know that and all police officers know that, but the Home Office doesn't see it our way. They never give us enough men to achieve our ideals. So we must make do with what we have and we can't halt what some regard as progress, Rhea,' he drained his mug. 'So we do as we are told. We've always done that, we police officers, even if it means being subordinate to a senior officer who is a woman. Well, I've got that off my chest so what are your plans for today?'

'I shall return to Aidensfield, Sergeant, and I'll probably do a foot patrol in the village. Meet a few people, chat to a few of the locals, make enquiries about Claude Jeremiah Greengrass to find out what he's up to these days ...'

'Well, don't let me keep you, Rhea.' He rose from the chair and returned to his office. It was time for me to depart too. As I was leaving, Alf Ventress entered to begin his shift in the office; his first chore would be the washing-up!

'Hello, Nick. Did you have a nice leave?'

'We rented a cottage near Ullswater,' I told him. 'It was lovely, sheer peace – even with four youngsters!'

I told him about our family holiday. Then, nodding towards Blaketon's closed office door, he asked, 'And how's Mein Führer?'

'He's worrying about changes,' I smiled. 'He's been chatting to me about it – something's set him off. He seems to have a chip on his shoulder about women police inspectors.'

'It'll be the arrival of that new inspector,' smiled Alf. 'Fresh from the special course at the police college. Somebody said it was Christine Pollock; Blaketon thinks it's a woman who's coming to Strensford but it's a chap, Crispin Pollock is his name. He's due to start this morning.'

'No one's told Blaketon it's a feller, then?' I smiled.

'No, not yet. We thought we'd let him sweat a bit,' grinned Alf, lighting a cigarette as he took his chair. 'It'll be interesting to see the preparations he makes for "Christine" when she makes her first official visit! So you *have* missed all the news! Strensford's divisional boundaries have been extended to include Eltering and Ashfordly, which means we are answerable to Strensford's hierarchy. And we might be doing seaside patrols too! That new inspector's been brought in to modernize the system, so they say. He's coming to implement new ideas and procedures, our division's a sort of testing ground for changes at force level. We're to be used to see if the new ideas and changed boundaries will work in practice.'

'But Pollock only joined a few years ago!' I cried. 'He's got less service than me!'

'He's got less service than most of the bloody members of this force,' grimaced Alf. 'Five years. He's still wet behind the ears! He's only twenty-six years old ... Blaketon's old enough to be his father but he'll be telling Blaketon what to do! He'll be telling us all what to do ... I don't know what the force is coming to, Nick, really I don't.'

I left Ashfordly police station with a sense of foreboding. Those of us with a few years' service to our credit were always conscious of our lack of promotion, but in those days it was normal to be promoted to the rank of sergeant after some twelve or fifteen years in the job. Having reached the exalted heights of being a sergeant, promotion to inspector might follow after a further five or six years – if one had passed the promotion exams. But this Pollock had passed his exams with very high marks, after which he'd spent a year at the police college on a course designed especially for those selected for accelerated promotion. And now he was back ... as a senior officer at Strensford. And he was to put into action a host of new, and probably very unpopular, changes. I shuddered.

But in spite of one's personal opinions and prejudices the job has to go on, and one of the blessings enjoyed by me was that Aidensfield was a fairly remote village. The fact meant it was well away from the constant supervision of senior officers. I was often left alone to get on with my job.

With a bit of luck and some applied ingenuity I could still work the beat in the way I thought best. At least, I hoped I could! I remembered one old constable who often said, 'Reforms are all right – so long as they don't change anything.' There were times and occasions when one could agree with that sentiment – and this was one of them!

★ ★ ★

I was mindful of the impending alterations to my mode of policing whilst going about my routine duties that summer. Working a rural beat as a police constable was a most pleasant means of earning a living, provided one was left alone to perform one's duties in one's own style. But when senior officers started to impose their own, often impracticable ideas, the routine quickly lost its appeal. Such an occasion occurred during the abnormally chilly, foggy and wet month of June that year.

I was patrolling Aidensfield on foot, enjoying the relaxed style of life in the village. I had parked the police van on the green and had spent the morning chatting to the locals, checking the homes of several old folk to see if they needed any help and visiting local businesses during the course of routine crime enquiries. Villains sometimes tried to offload their ill-gotten gains in village stores, for example, and these visits were all part of my routine enquiries. Besides, the sight of a uniformed bobby in a shop did act as a deterrent to shoplifters – and we did have shoplifters in Aidensfield!

Following these visits, I was walking towards the post office when a harassed-looking young woman ran up to me. In her early thirties, she was a sturdy young woman of medium build and had neat, dark hair cut short. She wore a light plastic raincoat and carried a small umbrella to ward off the persistent drizzle. I recognized her as Mrs Shaw, Joy to her friends, and it was very evident that she was in some distress.

'Oh, Mr Rhea, I'm glad I caught you. It's our Stephanie, I can't find her. I've looked everywhere ...'

'Shouldn't she be at school?' was my first reaction, knowing the girl to be eight or nine years old.

'Yes, but she never got there ... they rang me. Oh, I'm so worried ...'

'Come and sit in the van,' I said. 'We can talk there.'

In the warm shelter of the police minivan she explained how Stephanie had set off for Aidensfield primary school just after 8.30 this morning, her normal time. She'd been carrying a satchel containing some bird books because they were having a lesson about nature later in the day. Mrs Shaw had watched Stephanie walk to the end of the garden where she'd closed the gate behind herself as usual, waved and then hurried off to school. She had been wearing a yellow plastic mac with a hood. Mrs Shaw had then returned to the house to clear away the breakfast things and do her normal household chores.

The school had telephoned at half past ten to say Stephanie had not arrived. The headmistress, a Miss Blacker, had not been too concerned at first, thinking perhaps that Stephanie had been poorly, but when one of the other children said she'd seen her alone near the war memorial with her satchel, Miss Blacker had begun to experience some concern. The war memorial was not on Stephanie's direct route to school. A search of the school grounds and buildings had drawn a blank and so she'd called Stephanie's mother. Mrs Shaw explained how she had searched her own home with its bedrooms and outbuildings before going to her mother's house. Stephanie often went to visit her grandmother's cottage, especially after school, where she helped to feed the hens and geese, but granny had not seen her that morning. Joy Shaw added that she had searched all Stephanie's usual haunts but had not found any trace of the child.

Among the places she'd visited were the tennis club where Stephanie's mum often played (Mrs Shaw was secretary of the club), the village hall where she attended a junior youth club, the church hall where she went for her Brownie meetings and various other places in and around Aidensfield including the homes of her school friends. And now, having searched without success and having wept alone, she had found me. Her husband was a lorry driver and he was somewhere on the road in Northumberland well out of contact. Outside, she had put on a brave face but in the privacy of the police van she was weeping quietly to herself, a brave but very worried woman.

'Has she done this before?' I asked. 'Played truant, I mean?'

'No, never,' she said. 'She likes school, I've never had trouble getting her there. Today there was to be a nature lesson, and they were going on a walk beside the river this afternoon if it was fine. She was looking forward to that.'

'Did Mrs Blacker say if any other child was missing? I

mean, has she gone off with a playmate and forgotten the time, or what day it is? It can happen!'

'No, I asked. All the others are accounted for.'

'You know she was seen near the war memorial?' I put to her. 'Is there any reason why she should go that way?'

'None, I can't understand that. It's not on her way to school, I can't think why she would want to go that way.'

'She never said she was meeting anyone? A friend?'

'No, nothing,' wept Mrs Shaw.

The more I questioned Mrs Shaw about her own search for Stephanie, the more evident it was that the child's disappearance was both a mystery and a matter for concern. All the normal reasons for not attending school – bullying, a dislike of lessons, a dislike or fear of the teacher, inability to cope with reading or writing – had been considered and discounted. Stephanie was a clever child who loved school and who would never disappear like this under normal circumstances. This suggested the circumstances were not normal, which in turn demanded a fully co-ordinated search by professionals.

I drove Mrs Shaw home and together we searched the house yet again, this time with me opening the doors of wardrobes and cupboards, searching the loft, looking under beds and in outbuildings, checking the boot of the car and looking into dustbins and tea-chests plus a hundred and one other places where a child might hide but which an untrained searcher would never consider. I rang the school from Mrs Shaw's home too but the answer was still negative. Stephanie had not arrived.

The school and its buildings, along with all the other public and several private places, would have to be searched by police officers, but that demanded more officers and it would take a long time. I then decided to ring Sergeant Blaketon to ask him to mount an official search for Stephanie Shaw. By now it was just eleven o'clock in the morning and we had the whole day ahead of us, even if it was foggy, damp and dull.

From the office of my police house I rang Ashfordly police station. Alf Ventress answered. I explained the problem and he said, 'Hang on, Nick, Sergeant Blaketon's here.'

Blaketon came to the telephone and, upon hearing my account of events, said, 'Right, I'll ring Division and recruit some assistance. Police dogs will help, I'll request their attendance. We'll make a thorough search and I'm sure the villagers will help once word gets around. Meanwhile, Rhea, you take another recce around the village; check the school yourself and I'll meet you there in an hour. 12.30 at the school. Right?'

'Very good, Sergeant.'

While awaiting the sergeant and his team of searchers, I went to the school and searched the entire complex with Miss Blacker, indoors and out, and we drew a blank. Miss Blacker assured me that Stephanie was not a problem pupil, she enjoyed school and had lots of friends there. A little dreamy perhaps, but she was not bullied or teased by her classmates and the headmistress could think of no reason why the girl had not arrived this morning.

'You said she was a little dreamy?' I put to the teacher. 'What do you mean by that?'

'She lives in a world of her own sometimes. Day-dreaming I call it. Sometimes in class she will be concentrating on something in her head so much that she'll exclude everything that's going on around her. I just wondered if she'd wandered off in a bit of a dream this morning.'

'Has this caused problems before?' I asked.

'Not really,' smiled Miss Blacker. 'Although when she did a lesson about Jesus walking on the water, she went down to the river to try it. I think she thought she was Jesus!'

'She fell in?'

'No, the minute the cold water got into her shoes, she stopped – it was almost like snapping out of a trance. She does have a very strong imagination.'

'So what lessons did you do yesterday? Anything that might have promoted a similar reaction?'

'No, I did consider that but it was a very ordinary day of reading, writing and arithmetic.'

This snippet of information was important, I considered, and I began to wonder whether Stephanie had undergone one of her strange experiences before disappearing. It was

something I must pursue and something I must put to her
mother. Still at school, however, I found one of Stephanie's
friends who had seen her this morning. She was called Carol
Hodges. After questioning the child, she told me she'd seen
Stephanie near the war memorial just after half past eight;
she'd been wearing her distinctive yellow macintosh with the
hood up.

'But if she was near the war memorial,' I put to her,
'Stephanie must have been walking away from the school? Did
she say where she was going?'

'No,' said Carol. 'I said I would walk to school with her but
she said no, she'd catch me up.'

'Catch you up?'

'I sometimes walked to school with her from her house but
she was going the other way today. She just said she would
catch me up.'

'Did she say anything else? Who she was going to meet, or
where she was going? Why she was at the war memorial
perhaps?'

'No, she didn't say anything.'

'Was she going to the shops, maybe?'

'I don't know,' she said.

'So what did you do?'

'I went to school. When Stephanie didn't come, I told Miss
Blacker where I'd seen her.'

Miss Blacker interrupted now. 'That's when I became
rather concerned, Mr Rhea, and rang Joy Shaw.'

'Was anyone with her?' I had to ask Carol, 'A man or
woman, another boy or girl? A car maybe?'

'No, she was all by herself.'

'Was there a car or a lorry anywhere nearby?'

'No, nothing. She was just standing there all by herself.'

'Did you see where she went from the war memorial?'

Carol shook her head. 'It was drizzly and I had my hood up,
I just came to school and went straight inside.'

Having elicited as much information as I could from Carol,
I then addressed the entire class of children and asked if any of
them had seen Stephanie this morning. Two small boys had
seen her walking towards the war memorial and their sightings

confirmed Carol's version. But as all had been heading away from the distinctive stone cross, none had seen where she had gone from that point. The fact that she had walked to the war memorial was odd because it did not lie on her route from home to the school. To reach it, she had to make a considerable detour – if she had gone straight to school from there it would have added five or ten minutes to her normal journey.

I decided to ask at the nearby shops before Blaketon arrived; surely some of the shopkeepers had seen the child in her bright yellow raincoat and carrying her satchel. All those whom I questioned said that Mrs Shaw had been asking earlier in the morning and only one of the storekeepers had seen the child; he'd not been able to recognize her but had seen a little girl in a bright yellow raincoat standing near the war memorial just after 8.30. Like the other witnesses, he had not seen her leave that point.

As I heard these stories, there was a growing dread in my mind that she had been picked up by a passing vehicle. If that had happened, then she was at great risk; we might even have a murder investigation on our hands. But even that possibility did not explain why she had walked to the war memorial, a diversion from her normal route to school. If the child had been in some kind of trance it might explain her actions, but this seemed a rather remote possibility.

Then Sergeant Blaketon's familiar little black car arrived and I went to meet him. He was alone, Alf Ventress being left in Ashfordly police office to man the telephones and radio.

'Anything further to report, Rhea?' he asked as he donned his cap and came towards me.

I provided an update on the recent information but had to say that the girl's disappearance was a total mystery. I did express the fear that she might have entered a motor vehicle although we had no description or sighting of one.

'Well,' he added, 'Division say the new inspector's coming out to lead the search. She's going to use police college techniques with maps and compasses and things.'

'Hadn't we better get started?' I asked. 'The child's been missing for nearly four hours ...'

'Orders are orders, Rhea, and if our new inspector says we must wait for her arrival, then wait we must.'

'Did she say that herself?' I put to him.

'No, it was Division, relaying orders. "Inspector Pollock will rendezvous with you at the village school" was what they said. "At 12.50." Twenty minutes to go, that's all. What I want to know is how these young women police inspectors can improve the way we operate, Rhea. God, it's going to be tough. I'll be glad when I reach retiring age.'

'She might not be quite what you think, Sergeant,' I ventured, allowing him to continue thinking Pollock was female.

'She could be worse,' he added. To occupy the time before the arrival of Inspector Pollock I gave Sergeant Blaketon a guided tour of the school, re-examining all the places I had searched and introducing him to Miss Blacker. He repeated all the questions I had previously asked, and assured her that we would make every effort to find the child.

Then we went outside and he stood nervously beside the school gate, awaiting his new boss. A smart black police car appeared in the distance, followed by a personnel carrier containing ten constables and another sergeant.

'Here comes the cavalry,' he grunted. 'Led by Boadicea.'

Sergeant Blaketon was clearly nervous; he fidgeted with his feet and flicked imaginary specks of dust from his uniform as the little procession approached. Eventually the leading car turned into the parking space before the school and came to a halt. Inside, the outline of a figure in police uniform could be seen collecting documents, placing a cap on its head and checking its appearance in the driving mirror.

'She looks a bit on the bloody masculine side to me,' whispered Blaketon. 'Short hair cut ... wide shoulders ...'

As his gaze was concentrated upon the new inspector, the personnel carrier came to rest beside the car and its assortment of constables disembarked, led by the sergeant. By this stage, news of Stephanie's disappearance had circulated among the villagers and a small knot of bystanders began to assemble. In the meantime, the school had broken for lunch and the children were in the playground, shrieking and shouting as only a playground full of children is able. Miss Blacker, the only teacher in the small school, came across to join us. She asked if the children could help in the forthcoming search, but we declined; we didn't want more of them getting lost!

But Sergeant Blaketon's eyes were upon the inspector, now leaving the car. I watched Blaketon watching the inspector; the expression on his face became a frown as he realized that this was indeed a very mannish person; short hair, sturdy walk, the frame of a man and not a woman; wearing trousers, not a skirt.

'It is a man, Rhea! That new woman inspector is a man!'

'Yes, Sergeant,' I said. 'It looks very masculine to me.'

'Who said it was a woman?' he hissed from the side of his mouth.

'You did,' I replied.

'Me?'

'Yes, Sergeant, Christine Pollock, you said. It's actually Crispin Pollock …'

'Crispin? What sort of name is that?'

'He's the patron saint of cobblers, Sergeant,' I replied. 'St Crispin that is, not Inspector Pollock.'

'Cobblers?' he smiled wryly.

'And the same to you, Sergeant,' I returned as the new inspector came forward. Sergeant Blaketon and I each slung a crisp and smart salute and chanted, 'Good afternoon, sir,' as Inspector Pollock approached with a large map in his hand.

He was a short, rather squat individual with a very neatly cut head of light brown hair; his uniform was immaculate and his shoes were polished so that they reflected the dull light of the day. His face was rounded and plump, almost childlike in the clear state of his skin; it looked as if he had not reached the stage of shaving because his skin was soft and pink and his eyes were a light blue. It was a baby-face, I realized, but when he smiled his teeth were pure white and evenly positioned, and there was a look of genuine pleasure on his features.

'Sergeant Blaketon, I presume?' were his first words. 'And PC Rhea?'

'Yes, sir,' we chanted in unison.

'Good, well, let's get moving. There is no time to waste on

pleasantries. I have brought reinforcements from Strensford and the dog section is en route. Now, Sergeant, what have you discovered to date? We need a description of the missing child and then we can commence the search. We will quarter off the village and its surrounds, as per this large-scale map, and I will co-ordinate the search, using techniques I studied at the Police College. My car will be the control point; we have field radios and other equipment in the personnel carrier and loudhailers to maintain contact with any civilian volunteers who join us. Now, PC Rhea, you have made enquiries in the village? And you have made a perfunctory search?'

'It was more than that,' I had to tell him. 'It was a careful search, sir, done with the intention of examining all the likely hiding places in and around her home, her school and the key points of Aidensfield. It was thorough but it produced no results. She was last seen at the war memorial at half past eight and ...'

'It will be repeated,' was all he said. 'Now, I will explain how I propose to search the district, including the school, her home and every building in Aidensfield, then we shall expand into the outlying fields, moors and woods.'

'It's very foggy and wet, sir,' warned Sergeant Blaketon. 'Visibility in the woods and on the moors will be extremely limited and we shall have to exercise the utmost care when despatching our searchers. We don't want them to get lost.'

'The police college system allows for such problems, Sergeant. Right, men, gather around. And any volunteers – please join in.'

Inspector Pollock was clearly enjoying the challenge; on his very first day of duty he was able to put theory into practice in a most public way. He was showing no sign of nervousness or lack of experience. He was putting on a very confident show and I must admit I was impressed by his initial action. As he was speaking to his team of men a handful of villagers had gathered, among them Mrs Shaw, and they were ushered closer by a constable. Having made the introductory remarks and explained the task that lay ahead, Inspector Pollock outlined his plan of action. As he spoke, Claude Jeremiah Greengrass and Alfred, his lurcher dog, materialized from the fog. They stood at the back to listen. I saw Claude whispering to Mrs Shaw.

Inspector Pollock suggested that each constable be accompanied by at least two volunteers from the village. Then, laying his open map on the car bonnet, he proceeded to allocate areas for each group to search. He began with the imported constables. As he was performing this task, Greengrass sidled around to my side. Mrs Shaw came with him.

He whispered, 'A minute of your time, Mr Rhea.'

'I hope it's important, Claude,' I said. 'We're about to start an urgent search.'

'Well you'll need to begin with Beckside Woods,' grunted Claude. 'I saw that lass there this morning, nine o'clockish, in her yellow mac. I've just been asking Joy about her ...'

'What was she doing there?' I asked.

'Heading deep into t'woods,' said Claude.

I turned to Mrs Shaw. 'Joy, why would she go into the woods?'

The tearful Mrs Shaw shook her head. 'I can't say, I've no idea ... we've been there for walks, with Stephanie, but she's never mentioned going there alone, certainly not this morning.'

I then decided to ask Mrs Shaw about Stephanie's alleged day-dreaming and her mother confirmed this. 'Oh yes, she gets so wrapped up in things. When she read *Alice in Wonderland*, she went out looking for the White Rabbit and the entrance to Wonderland, and ...'

'Joy,' I put to her. 'What did she read last night? Or perhaps she watched television? What was on?'

'There was a repeat of that old film, *The Adventures of Robin Hood*, you know, the 1938 version with Errol Flynn. She was absorbed by that, the men in Lincoln green, their lives in the woods and so on.'

'That's it,' said Claude quietly. 'There is a Robin Hood's Cave in those woods of ours.'

'My husband said something about that!' and for the first time there was a smile on Joy Shaw's face. 'During the film, he said he'd tried to find Robin Hood's Cave in Beckside Woods when he was a small boy, and he never did find it! He mentioned a legend about a tunnel going to Robin Hood's Bay ... yes, I remember him saying that ... I bet Stephanie heard him ...'

'Where is this cave, Claude?' I asked him.

'Well,' he said, blinking his eyes rapidly. 'There's a few, six or eight caves, and all of 'em said to be where Robin Hood rested. The genuine one has an underground passage leading to Robin Hood's Bay, so they say; he used it as an escape route when the authorities were after him.'

'Do you know where they are?' I asked. 'And have you used that tunnel when the authorities have been pressing you?'

'Well, there's no tunnel, that's just a tale. But as to where the caves are, well, I might know and I might not, I mean, it's not as if I go trespassing on private land, Mr Rhea. Them woods are private, you know, they're on Lord Ashfordly's estate.'

'Come off it, Claude! Stop being so defensive – and besides, there is a public right of way through the woods. But this is serious, you're not breaching your principles to help the police, you're helping the people of Aidensfield to find a little girl.'

'Aye, well, if you put it like that. Right, well, I know where most of 'em are, they're just caves, you know, holes in the rock, nowt special about 'em.'

And so it was decided to abandon Inspector Pollock's wider plan of action in order to concentrate upon the woodland caves. His map did show the woodland and its paths, of which there were several, and he began to divide the wood into areas, each of which would be searched by a team of police and civilian volunteers. A constable would remain at the car for radio contact and the rest of us would search the four square miles or so of Beckside Wood. To search the caves, we were issued with electric torches from the personnel carrier, but it was decided that the field radios would be an encumbrance – besides, they'd probably not function over the distance between the village and the wood. Mrs Shaw asked if she could come, but we suggested not.

'You'll be far better at home,' suggested Pollock. 'If

Stephanie does return home, she'll want you there, won't she? Not in the wilds of the North York Moors looking for her!'

'Yes, of course. But the moment you know something ...'

'We'll let you know,' smiled Pollock.

And so the massive search began. Carrying a map in a waterproof cover and strung around his neck like a rambler, Inspector Pollock marshalled his troops and allocated them each a section of the wood. Sergeant Blaketon and Sergeant Lazenby from Strensford were each given half of the wood to supervise while the constables' task was to search the undergrowth as well as any caves, just in case the child had fallen and injured herself. In addition to the torches we were equipped with long sticks with which to probe the undergrowth.

Claude Jeremiah, with his unrivalled knowledge of the countryside, directed each of the groups to their positions. I found myself with two village men and we were allocated a portion of woodland beneath the towering cliffs through which the river flowed; it was on the Elsinby edge of the wood, about a mile from Aidensfield.

As we trudged towards the venue, Claude Jeremiah caught us and said, 'I'd better show you this cave, Mr Rhea, it takes a bit of finding, it's hidden with undergrowth and the entrance is nobbut the size of a dog kennel door. But inside, it's like a ballroom ...'

Without elaborating the detail of that search, it is sufficient to say that we found the cave and that I would never have located it without the aid of Claude Jeremiah. Even as he led us to the tiny entrance, we could see the curled-up figure of a little girl in a bright yellow raincoat. She was just inside the cave, lying asleep on a bed of dry leaves.

'Stephanie?' I touched her gently and she awoke with a smile. 'Come along, time to go home.'

'I came to find Robin Hood's Cave,' she said.

'And you've found it,' I said. 'Come along ...'

'I wanted to look inside but it was dark,' she spoke sadly. 'I had no torch.'

I looked at Claude and the other men, then said, 'OK, I've got a torch, come along, we'll have a look inside, all of us.'

And so we crawled into the dark interior, squeezing through the tiny entrance. As I switched on the torch I realised that Claude had been right. It was massive inside; shining the light on the walls, I reckoned it was as large as the average village church and then, as the torch swept along the dusty, web-ridden walls, Stephanie shouted,

'There it is ... look!'

I halted my action and moved the circle of light back a few yards. And there, hanging on a narrow protruding piece of rock was a quiver of arrows and a long bow. Reaching up, it was just possible to reach down the bow and the quiver; each item was smothered in dust, probably from centuries past. None of us could speak.

'I don't believe it,' I whispered.

'She does,' smiled Claude.

'Here,' I said to Stephanie. 'You can take these home – then everyone will know you were the person who found Robin Hood's Cave.'

Following the successful search, we reassembled at the school as, one by one, the searchers emerged dripping and wet from the woodland. It was still foggy but everyone had been recalled and the sergeants were ticking off the names. Mrs Shaw hurried out to meet us, somebody having telephoned her to say we were emerging from the woods with Stephanie safe and sound. Soon we were all gathered before the school; George from the pub had managed to produce some mugs of warm soup and some bread buns. Then Sergeant Blaketon asked, 'Where's the inspector?'

Sergeant Lazenby did a quick count of heads, shouting out the names of his constables. Each one responded.

'That man hasn't got himself lost, has he?' grinned Sergeant Blaketon.

'If he has, I'm not looking for him!' smirked Claude Jeremiah. 'I don't believe in helping the police!'

'Has anyone seen the inspector?' Blaketon called to the assembled officers.

'He was supervising the entire operation, somewhere deep in the trees,' volunteered one constable. 'He had his map ...'

'Well, he's not come out of the trees,' Blaketon observed

wryly, and added, 'Rhea! This is your patch, so it is your responsibility. You'd better go back into those woods and find the inspector! In the meantime, we will wait here and drink our soup!'

'Yes, Sergeant,' I acknowledged. The inspector had a loudhailer with him but its range was limited; I took another with me hoping I could make contact by bellowing through the thing. I could imagine myself shouting 'Inspector Pollock' in the dense woodland. But I knew the team would be waiting when I emerged – if I emerged! I hoped I didn't get lost in that dripping thick fog.

But as I trudged back into the damp and foggy woodland, I found myself forgetting about the inspector – all I could think about was that bow and the quiver of arrows which had been hanging in Robin Hood's Cave.

2   Tricks in Every Trade

That one may smile and smile and be a villain.
William Shakespeare (1564–1616)

There are very few criminals who will boast about their activities to the police but Samuel James Carson was such a man. Although he lived a long way from Aidensfield, in York to be precise, he was known to most of the officers in the police forces across the north of England. Criminal intelligence circulars warned us about his activities and although we maintained a careful watch for him during his law-breaking, he always managed to evade capture. He was a master criminal without a criminal record. We knew that. The public didn't.

In his early thirties when I was at Aidensfield, Samuel James Carson was a highly professional housebreaker and burglar. He featured in many of our sectional meetings and conferences at Ashfordly police station, and he was the topic of a good deal of police gossip, but I had never met him. Even so, I felt I knew him well because his activities were such a regular feature of our crime circulars and discussions.

Although his speciality was breaking into domestic dwelling-houses, he would occasionally switch to garages, inns or shops – all places where cash was kept.

At that time, prior to 1968, breaking into a house during the daytime hours (i.e. between 6am and 9pm) was called housebreaking, while breaking into a house at night (i.e. between 9pm and 6am) was known as burglary. Burglary was then considered a most serious crime, on a level with robbery and rape. At one time burglary carried the death penalty and even in the 1960s the penalty was a maximum of life imprisonment. At that time, there were very few cases of burglary! By comparison, housebreaking resulted in a maximum penalty of fourteen years' imprisonment if theft or some other crime was also committed within the premises, and seven years if the breaking was done merely with the *intention* of committing a theft or other serious crime inside the house.

A range of lesser crimes included warehouse-breaking, schoolhouse-breaking, garage-breaking, shop-breaking, office-breaking and so forth. Also regarded as a very serious crime was sacrilege: i.e. breaking into a church or other place of divine worship; this had also once carried the death penalty but during the 1960s the maximum penalty was life imprisonment.

The Theft Act 1968 altered the entire law relating to breaking into premises and all such crimes were collectively known as burglary, irrespective of the type of premises which was attacked. The penalty for burglary was reduced to a maximum of fourteen years, with life imprisonment for aggravated burglary, i.e. committing burglary while armed with a firearm, explosive or other weapon of offence.

Few burglars now receive anything like the maximum penalty – a period of probation or a fine (often paid by further burglaries) is the normal penalty. And, of course, all breaking offences have multiplied considerably during the past thirty years or so.

But neither the then severe punishment for burglary nor the tough penalties for house-breaking deterred Samuel James Carson from his chosen career. He burgled merrily in and around York and was able to afford a modest but very smart car. I think he could have purchased a very splendid model, but he seemed content with what might be described as a family saloon. Thus equipped, he travelled into the outlying towns and villages to continue his profession, burgling by night and house-breaking by day.

At that time, before the age of the computer, police stations maintained an index of criminals and their activities and we were able to identify most of those who were active. We were aware of the criminals who were operating on our patch, even if the courts refused to convict them. In the ever-present hope that, one day, we would be able to provide the villains with the punishment they deserved, we kept them under observation and noted their movements. In our efforts to secure a conviction, we relied on real evidence (i.e. being caught in possession of the stolen goods) although good circumstantial evidence would always help to secure a conviction if a defence lawyer was as crooked as the villains.

It was in this way that officers in the police forces surrounding York maintained their surveillance of Samuel James Carson. Our officers knew what he was doing; they stopped his car and searched him many many times, but not once did they produce the evidence necessary to convict him. People might ask how police officers know a person is committing crime when such a person has never been convicted; the answer is that police officers are professionals. Just as an artist knows instinctively when a picture is right, and when a hair dresser knows a hair-style is right without being able to explain why, so a police officer knows who is committing crimes.

Proving such knowledge to the satisfaction of a modern court of law is, however, very difficult and sometimes impossible. But police officers do know who the criminals are, and they know the damage and destruction these parasites can cause to society. And one such parasite was Samuel James Carson. Certainly, he did not regard himself or his activities as offensive in any way. He regarded himself as a professional person, a man whose skills lay in taking money from others in much the same way that shops, bookmakers or dealers take money from their customers. Our intelligence system indicated that he did not think he was being sinful, wrong or even selfish even if he was breaking the law. He knew he was breaking the law, but he did not believe his activities were wrong.

House-breaking and burglary provided his livelihood and he considered himself the best in his chosen profession. In that, he was probably correct. To his credit, he never carried a firearm, he never used violence against any person or animal, he never raided the homes of the sick or the aged and he would never offer any kind of violence towards the police. He was far too much of a gentleman to lower himself to that kind of behaviour. Furthermore, he never stole jewellery or objects of sentimental value; his only objective was bank notes. Coins were too bulky and noisy to carry away, so he never stole anything but paper money. He never caused damage in the houses he raided, other than a small hole in a ground-floor window or the glass panel of a door. He did this so that he could reach inside and release the window catch or door lock, and so let himself in.

Sometimes, he would borrow a ladder from the garage of his intended target and climb through a bedroom window. One of his boasts was that his 'customers' always supplied him with the means of entry – this might include a small brick or stone to smash the glass, a ladder to gain access upstairs, a key left inside a lock or on a piece of string inside the letter box or even under the doormat, a chisel, screwdriver or some other tool in a garden shed to force a stubborn window. Garden spades were ideal for lifting patio doors from their rails, for example.

Samuel James never carried house-breaking tools because his customers were good enough to provide them. Some even helped by advertising their absence – they did this through milk deliveries not being cancelled, newspapers being delivered and left sticking out of the letter box for days on end, lights not showing during dark evenings and similar evidence of a deserted house. He always said his customers made his job that much easier. And so they did.

But to see him walking around the streets, one would never guess he was a criminal. In appearance he was like any other professional person – he might have been a doctor, a solicitor, an accountant, a bank manager or even a high-grade salesman. He was of average height, something around five feet nine inches, and was always clean and tidy. His dark brown hair was cut in the fashion of the period, he wore smart dark business-type suits, polished black shoes and often carried a brief-case.

Whenever the police searched him or his case, there was never any evidence of his burgling activities. The brief-case might contain a map or even his sandwiches, never any house-breaking tools or evidence of his crimes.

He drove a clean, smart but modest car which he changed
frequently – his cars were always of average appearance like a
Ford Cortina, Hillman Minx or a modest Vauxhall and his
only hobby was horse-racing. Through that he could, if the
occasion demanded (such as an income tax investigation),
explain his cash income.

Carson's confidence in his own infallibility was such that he
would boast openly to the police, and even to people like
shopkeepers and landlords, of his criminal activities. Even on
holiday, when people quizzed him about his job, he would say
he was a professional burglar. Few believed him. We knew he
did this because he once told a man he met in the Lake
District; the man happened to be an off-duty police officer
who quietly passed on the details of Carson's whereabouts at
that time.

Among his claims was that he had bought his terrace house
in York with the proceeds of crime; he bought his clothes,
food and furnishings with cash from the same source and in
fact, every penny he spent was the proceeds of crime. But
because it was all in cash, taken from houses all over the north
of England, it was impossible to prove the origin of the
money. Few people kept a list of their bank-note serial
numbers and so there was no proof that the source of his cash
was illegal.

We, the police, knew where it was coming from, but we
could never prove it.

Like all local officers, I regularly received circulars about
his activities; we were even treated to a black-and-white
photograph of him in several police publications. But, to my
knowledge, Samuel James Carson had never ventured across
the moors to Aidensfield yet. I was always vigilant, knowing
that one day – or more likely, one night – he might arrive.

I fully expected him to target the village for one of his raids
because there were some good-quality dwelling-houses in the
vicinity, many owned by people who kept a lot of cash on the
premises. The one thing I did not anticipate, however, was
that he would actually buy a cottage and move into the village
as one of the residents. But that is precisely what he did.

At first, I did not associate the Mr Carson who bought No 2

Hilltop Terrace with Samuel James Carson, the burglar from York. The house, a neat stone-built three-bedroomed property with a nice garden and garage, had been on the market for a few weeks and it was George Ward at the pub who told me it had been sold.

'It's a businessman from York who's bought it,' he told me one morning. 'A smart-looking young chap, self-employed businessman, he said he was. He said he'd always wanted a cottage in the country and this place was ideal; quiet, off the beaten track, plenty of room inside, not overlooked, recently modernized. He paid cash, an' all, no mortgage, so he must be earning good money.'

'Do you know him at all, George?' I was always interested in newcomers to Aidensfield.

George shook his head. 'No, I can't say I do. He came in here for a drink and a sandwich once or twice when he was considering buying the cottage. He looked around it a few times with the estate agent before he made his mind up. Carson, he said his name was.'

'Decent sort of fellow, was he?' I asked.

'Yes, very. A real pleasant young chap, the sort we could do with in Aidensfield.'

Even though George had supplied me with the man's name, I must admit I did not immediately associate it with Samuel James Carson. Then, in due course, Carson moved into the house. I saw a small removal van parked outside one morning, but no sign of the new owner. I did not intrude – after all, there was no reason. Then, about a week later, I was on patrol one morning when I small a small green Austin car at the garage. A smart young man was buying some petrol and when he handed over the cash, I saw his face. I knew I had seen it somewhere before and when I heard the petrol pump attendant say, 'Thank you, Mr Carson,' I realized who was now living on my patch.

My heart sank. It was Samuel James Carson, the north's most successful house-breaker, burglar and full-time criminal. I must admit I was in a momentary quandary and before I could decide what action I should take, he jumped into his car and drove out of the village. I did, however, have time to note the registration number.

A check with the vehicle taxation department would confirm the name of the owner – just in case it wasn't the Carson in whom I had some professional interest! I returned to my police house and rang the taxation department at Northallerton. They supplied the name of the owner of the car.

It was indeed Samuel James Carson of 2 Hilltop Terrace, Aidensfield. A man who never overlooked the smallest detail, he had immediately registered his new address with the vehicle taxation department. That one small action by him made me realise he was a man to be reckoned with; quite clearly, he thought of everything to avoid confrontation with the law, so to convict him of a crime was never going to be easy.

My next task was to break the glad tidings to Sergeant Blaketon. I rang the office at Ashfordly. He was there.

'Good morning, Sergeant,' I greeted him. 'I've got some very interesting news for you.'

'I hope it's good news,' he sniffed. 'I could do with some good news. I think I've got the flu.'

'Well, this should clear your head,' I laughed. 'You remember those circulars about Samuel James Carson, the York burglar?'

'Yes?' There was a question in his voice.

'We're all supposed to keep a look-out for him,' I strung him along. 'To report sightings and so forth for the CID, so that the Crime Squad can monitor his movements ...'

'Rhea, are you trying to tell me that Samuel James Carson has just driven through Aidensfield?' he sniffed.

'No, Sergeant. I'm reporting that he's just bought a house in Aidensfield. He's coming to live here, he's one of my villagers now; he's one of the residents of this village whose life and property I must protect.'

'I don't like jokes, Rhea!' he snapped.

'It's no joke, Sergeant. But as he is now resident on my patch, I thought I'd better report his presence amongst us.'

'You can't be serious, Rhea! I don't believe this ... I can do without this right now. What makes you so sure it's him?'

'I recognized him, Sergeant. He's got a car, I've checked the registration number. He's bought a cottage at No 2 Hilltop Terrace, Aidensfield, and he paid cash for it. His car's an Austin,' and I gave him the registration number.

'And that'll mean a crime wave hereabouts, Rhea, a crime wave that never gets halted and crimes that never get solved. I can do without this ...'

'You sound as if you're sick ...'

'I am now!' He coughed.

'Take a few days off, Sergeant,' I suggested. 'We could always hand over this responsibility to the new inspector.'

'I can cope, Rhea, no sprog inspector's going to show me how to deal with a criminal of this kind. An inspector who gets himself lost in the woods will be no good at logging the movements of the most notorious criminal since Dick Turpin.'

'So, what do I do about it, Sergeant?' I asked him.

'Nothing for the time being, Rhea, just keep an eye on him. Make a note of his every move, dates, times and places he resorts to. Get the names and personal descriptions of anybody who calls on him, and log their car numbers.' He sniffed.

'Very good, Sergeant.'

'Note the times he leaves at night to go about his nefarious trade, list the dealers he might be visiting, anything that will nail him. We'll show those other forces how to deal with real villains, Rhea, mark my words,' and he sneezed violently.

'But what about telling CID and the Crime Squad?'

'Leave that to me, Rhea, and by the way ...'

'Sergeant?'

'It was good work, Rhea, very observant of you. It's vital that a good country constable knows his patch and everyone who lives and works upon it. Especially the villains. Good work. I'm sure our new inspector will be impressed.'

And so the arrival of Samuel James Carson was duly recorded in the crime intelligence system of Ashfordly Section. The problem was what to do about him. I realized that I would have to meet him face-to-face sooner or later and decided that the best approach would be for me to make the first move. I would pay him a visit at his house and introduce myself.

When I made my first call that same morning, he was out. I knew that his car number would already have been circulated to

neighbouring police forces and all officers on patrol in our own
area. That meant his vehicle would be stopped and searched if
it was seen. I peeped through the window of the cottage.
Inside it was neatly but sparsely furnished. There was a TV set
in one corner, some nice vases and china ornaments, paintings
on the wall and a clean rug before the fireplace. A typical home
in fact. I knew none of these items would have been stolen – he
was too crafty for that because some of them, like the TV set,
might be identifiable by serial numbers or other marks. But all
this would have been paid for with stolen money – and there
was no way anyone could prove that.

Eventually, one afternoon, I did find him at home. I
knocked on his door and he opened it with a smile.

'Come in, PC Rhea,' he held the door wide open. 'Nice to
make your acquaintance.'

He spoke with barely a trace of a local accent and pointed to
a chair. 'Drink?' he asked. 'Tea, coffee? Something stronger?'

'No thanks,' I refused, knowing that a man of this calibre
could construe my acceptance of even a cup of tea as being a
bribe or at least a tacit acceptance of his criminal way to life.

'So what brings the law to my humble home?' he asked.

'You are Samuel James Carson?' I tried to make my visit
sound very formal.

'The very same,' he smiled charmingly. 'Recently arrived
from York. Very happy to settle in Aidensfield. A lovely part
of the country, charming place.'

'You are aware that we know how you earn your living?' I
felt it unwise to accuse him outright of being a criminal.

'Of course,' the same warm smile crossed his face. 'You
know your job, you are doing it very well, you are a
professional which is why you are here now. I am a
professional too, Mr Rhea; I know your name for a start. I
know that your people are watching me, hoping to catch me as
I go about my work. But they never will. I am a professional
burglar, Mr Rhea, the best there is. I steal only cash and I will
never break into any premises in this village. That is one of my
rules – never commit crimes on my own doorstep. In York, I
lived in Bootham and never burgled that part of the city. I will
not harm a living thing, Mr Rhea, I will take only cash and

you will never catch me. I shall live a peaceful, quiet and fulfilled life in this village; I shall never harm a hair of anyone's head and I shall not be a threat to you or to anyone here. I am a self-employed man who will leave the village to go to work, just like any other commuter.'

'If you weren't a self-confessed burglar, I should welcome you,' I told him. 'But I can't make you welcome, not when you admit to being a burglar.'

'Well, that's put the record straight,' that smile was still there. 'It's a pity we couldn't be friends, two professionals who each respect the other's skills.'

'I can never respect a criminal,' I said. 'My job is to apprehend those who commit crime.'

'And for that you need proof, eh? You will never get proof that I am a housebreaker or burglar, Mr Rhea. Never.'

'I can always try,' I said.

'Others have tried in the past,' he said. 'Senior detectives, crime squad officers, uniformed patrols, traffic police ... I shall never be caught, Mr Rhea. You are wasting your time.'

'I came here just to let you know I am aware of your identity and your mode of life.' I stood up to leave. 'I came also to let you know that I shall not cease in my attempts to convict you of any crime you might commit.'

'Fair enough. I respect your honesty. And I shall tell you that I will continue to commit housebreakings and burglaries throughout the north of England, but not in Aidensfield. Catch me if you can, Mr Rhea.'

And on that note, I left his house.

I knew that I was to be faced with regular night patrols during which I would have to stop and search Carson or his vehicle; I would also have to ring the CID to warn of his departure from the village, knowing that if he intended going to Middlesbrough for the evening he would make us believe he was heading for Harrogate or Scarborough or even Leeds. He was clever, he was cunning. I guessed that when he stole cash, he did so in small quantities – £10 here, £5 there, small sums taken on spec from handbags left on kitchen tables, insurance money tucked into tea caddies, milk money left on doorsteps. And then he would hide it overnight, or pay it into a bank account or into a post office savings account so that we never caught him with large sums upon him. I guessed we never knew the extent of his crimes. If he had a day in Middlesbrough, stealing from houses with unlocked doors as neighbours gossiped, I guessed he might pick up £100 in small sums without anyone realizing he'd even paid a visit. £5 missing here, or £1 there or even a ten-shilling note might not be missed if the house bore no signs of forcible entry. The police might not even be informed of the majority of these crimes.

Over supper after my first visit, I told Mary about him and she asked, 'But you could have accepted a cup of tea from him, surely?'

'No,' I said. 'Not from him.'

'But why?'

'Because if the tea leaves were bought with stolen money, then they also become stolen property,' I tried to explain the law. 'And if I knew the property was stolen and then received it myself, I would be guilty of receiving stolen property. I know it would never be proved, but that is the principle of the law. With a man like Carson, I must not give him one tiny hint that I sanction his lifestyle. Not the tiniest of hints.'

'But that means that when he buys anything at all, the people who take his money are guilty of receiving stolen property.'

'Not necessarily,' I said. 'They don't *know* the money is stolen. I do.'

'But if you told them he was living by crime,' she smiled, 'then they would know. Then they would be guilty of receiving stolen property.'

And I knew she had provided me with the ideal means of making Carson's life intolerable, at least in Aidensfield. I started at the garage.

'Malcolm,' I said to the owner. 'That new chap, Carson. He gets petrol here?'

'Yes, he said he'd be using quite a lot, he travels all over, he said.'

'He's a professional burglar and house-breaker.' I told him all about Carson. 'He boasts about it. Which means his cash is stolen money – which means you are receiving stolen money, doesn't it? And if you know it's stolen, you are liable to be arrested and charged with receiving stolen money.'

'Stolen money? I had no idea it was stolen ...'

'But you know now, Malcolm,' I smiled. 'And I want you to tell everyone else, just as I'm going to do. The shop, the butcher, the post office, George at the pub, shops, garages, pubs and post offices in Ashfordly. Elsinby, Maddleskirk, Thackerston, Briggsby, Crampton and in fact throughout the entire district. I'll stop him spending his money, Malcolm.'

'Aye, well, I've no wish to find myself in court,' said Malcolm.

I decided to emphasize my point. 'We're building a file on his activities,' I continued. 'Where he spends his cash, who his contacts are, where he goes by day and by night ...'

By the time I had finished, I knew that Malcolm would spread the word around his own colleagues, friends and contacts. They would all be frightened of accepting money from Carson. From there, I went across to the pub for a similar chat with George and then the post office, shop, butcher ...

Knowing how rapidly and effectively a village bush-telegraph system works, I realized that all the retailers would agree not to accept Carson's money, so I spent two or three days going around the other villages on my beat, repeating this exercise. I told Alf Ventress too, and he said he'd pass the word around Ashfordly, aided by the local constables. So we began our campaign against the charming Samuel James Carson.

It took a few days for him to realize what had happened and I was delighted one day, when he arrived at the garage while I was there, that Malcolm said he could not accept his cash. Carson looked at me.

'Every business in this area will refuse your money,' I smiled at him. 'They don't want to be charged with receiving stolen cash. You can't buy anything hereabouts, Mr Carson – no food, clothing, petrol ...'

'Is this your way of telling me to leave Aidensfield?' he smiled, but I could see that the smile was weak now. His eyes betrayed something of his concern.

'You can stay as long as you like,' I returned his smile. 'We're not like the Wild West, we don't drum people out of town. But none of the local tradespeople will take your money.'

'So you're saying I should sell up and move on?' The smile had gone.

'And who would buy a house that was bought with stolen money?' I asked him. 'Which estate agent would handle the sale of a house bought with stolen money, Mr Carson? It will be my duty to warn them, won't it? To prevent them committing a crime. And which furniture removal firm would help to remove furnishings bought with stolen cash?'

'You bastard,' he said, driving off. Now the charm had gone and so had the smile.

He moved out a week later (Malcolm actually gave him two gallons of petrol to help his departure) and he went to live in Newcastle upon Tyne, but the house remained unsold. No one would buy it and no one would rent it from him. Our efforts made sure of that. We rang the CID at Newcastle to warn them of his arrival and explained what we had done. Newcastle City Police said they would continue in a similar vein, although such action would be more difficult in a large town. But Samuel James Carson never returned to Aidensfield, not even to burgle one of our houses.

* * *

Aidensfield's best known criminal was, of course, Claude Jeremiah Greengrass and although he was not in the same league as Samuel James Carson, he was a petty nuisance. Claude wasn't evil – but he was very devious. Typical of his activities was the time he purchased a fine chest of mahogany drawers for just £1 from old Mrs Murphy. Although I was no expert in antiques, I had seen a similar chest for sale in Strensford for £250 and reckoned that hers was worth far more than a mere one pound.

I discovered this when I paid a routine visit to Mrs Rita Murphy; she lived by herself on a smallholding which she and her husband, Ted, had run. Ted had also worked for the county highways department until his death, and now Mrs Murphy was alone with her cottage and patch of land to care for. Whenever I was passing, I would pop in for a chat, just to see that she was all right. Hers was not an easy life and she was always short of cash, and so she would occasionally sell a piece of unwanted furniture or pottery. And Claude had scored with this purchase. Later, I discovered he had sold it to an antique shop in Strensford for £25.

'You were a bit sharp with Mrs Murphy,' I had to express my concern when I saw him in the village. 'A pound for those drawers, Claude! You could have given her £10 or even £15.'

'It's not breaking the law, Mr Rhea,' he blinked at me. 'Just a good bit of business, buy cheap and sell at a profit. That's how money is made, that's how I operate.'

'But she's a widow, Claude, she can't afford to let things go that cheap!'

'She's got a bit put by,' he was contemptuous of my concern. 'She's worth a fortune, with all that land and that house.'

'But she has no income, Claude. She'd only be well off if she sold up.'

'Aye, well, she's like me then. Existing from day to day like all us poor landowners, doing what we can to make ends meet ...'

I realized he had no conscience and gave up my efforts to make him repent. Claude was proud of his moment of success, regarding it as nothing more than a good business deal. I could take no action because he had not broken any law.

It would be several months later, as I called one morning during a routine visit, that I found her in some distress.

'What's wrong, Mrs Murphy?' I asked.

'Oh, I shouldn't trouble you with my worries, Mr Rhea,' she sighed. 'It's that paddock of mine, I was going to have it ploughed up and had decided to plant it with potatoes. I could make a few pounds selling them. I've bought the seed potatoes and Ron Lewis said he would plough it over for me – I'd pay him. Well, he's gone bankrupt, the receivers have impounded his gear and so he can't come. The others I've asked either charge too much or can't come for weeks.'

'It's urgent, is it?'

'Yes, it needs to be done soon, you see, if I'm to plant my

crop, I'll have to do it within the next couple of weeks. If I
don't, my seed potatoes will be wasted and I've laid good
money out for them, money I can ill afford.'

'It's not very large, is it? The paddock?' I asked.

'A shade over an acre.'

'If I can persuade someone to come and do it for nothing,
would you agree?' In the deep recesses of my mind I was
thinking about Claude Jeremiah Greengrass for I felt he had to
be made to pay for his earlier deception of this lady.

'For nothing? Nobody works for nothing these days, Mr
Rhea, not even for people like me!'

'Leave it with me,' I said. 'I'll be in touch – but if anyone
comes to offer to plough your land for nothing, don't be
surprised!'

I knew where to find Claude Jeremiah. He would be in the
pub at lunchtime and so I made it my purpose to pop in,
ostensibly for a casual chat with George and the regulars.
These pub visits were part of our duty, not only to check on
the good conduct of the premises, but also to gather crime
intelligence from local gossip. We never drank on duty,
however. Sure enough, as I entered the bar I saw Claude
Jeremiah and his cronies playing dominoes, each with a pint at
his side.

There were the usual pleasantries, combined with the usual
banter from Claude, then George asked,

'Anything doing in the big world outside these walls?' He
was pulling a foaming pint for Claude who now stood at my
side.

'I'm swotting up the law on treasure trove,' I smiled. 'I
reckon I might need to know the procedures soon.'

'Treasure?' cried George and this was enough to alert
Claude.

'I've just been to see old Rita Murphy up at Hollings
Intake,' I said. 'She's on about ploughing that paddock of hers
and setting it down with taties.'

'Everybody's planting taties these days!' smiled George.
'They keep the crisp factories going! It must be my turnover
of cheese and onion flavoureds!'

'What's this about a treasure then?' Claude could not resist.

'You'll probably know better than me,' I said to him. 'There was a tale, years ago, about a previous occupant of Hollings Intake. An old woman – she was called Hollings. She hid a hoard of gold sovereigns in a treacle tin somewhere in that paddock; then a man came along offering to buy sovereigns at £3 apiece – this was in the 1940s, I think, and she said she had some but they'd take a while to find. She told him to come back. He asked how many she had – he was thinking of buying two or three, but she said she had three or four *hundred*. He said he'd come back after he'd been to the bank!'

'Blimey!' exclaimed Claude. 'Four hundred sovereigns!'

'Anyway,' I continued. 'While he was away she got her spade out and began to dig, but she'd forgotten exactly where she'd buried the tin.'

'Get away!' George was listening intently.

'Before the chap returned she found three tins, all full of coins! She'd buried them so long ago she'd forgotten about them. She took four hundred out of the tins and kept them ready for the buyer – well, he came back with the cash and paid her £3 for each one. A handsome profit. £1,200 for an outlay of £400. And she still had several hundred left!'

'So what did she do with those she didn't sell?' asked Claude.

'She buried them again, separating the tins this time. And she put the money he'd paid in with the remaining sovereigns. Then she died and the story got forgotten, but somebody unearthed it in an old newspaper last week. I wish I'd kept the tale – so there's some full treacle tins of gold sovereigns and fivers somewhere under that soil, they reckon.'

'But doesn't Mrs Murphy know about it?' asked George, with Claude listening carefully.

'She didn't mention it to me,' I said. 'I don't think she knows the tale, it happened many years before she and her husband bought the place. I think I must pop around there later today and tell her. That's why I'm swotting up the law on treasure trove, just in case those tins turn up.'

'Are they likely to turn up?' asked George.

'If the field's given a good ploughing, they might,' I said. 'Or if somebody's read the story in the paper, they might turn up to start digging one night; she might lose the lot if the story gets widely publicized!'

'And if anybody found them, could they keep them?' George persisted.

'Well, it's possible,' I said. 'But the system is to report it to the police as treasure trove, then there'd be an inquest on the find.'

'Inquest?' said Claude.

'Yes, an enquiry conducted by the coroner. If he decides the money was deliberately hidden years ago, then it belongs to the state – but the finder gets the full market value. The finder, that is, not the landowner. The finder is paid the full market price and the gold coins would be handed to the British Museum.'

'So him that finds that money could be rich?' beamed Claude.

'It's a big field to dig by hand!' said George.

'Some folks have ploughs for that sort of thing!' I laughed. 'There's riches galore under our soil if only we could get at it.'

'Well,' Claude said suddenly. 'I must be off. I've work to do. Come on, Alfred,' he called to his lurcher. 'We can't sit around in this place when there's work to be done.'

When man and dog had rushed out, George asked, 'Where's he gone rushing off to? He hasn't finished his pint!'

'I think he'll be offering to plough Rita Murphy's paddock,' I smiled.

George looked at me. 'That tale about the gold,' he had a quizzical look on his face. 'Was it true?'

'It was – but it didn't happen anywhere near Mrs Murphy's paddock,' I smiled. 'It happened at Littlebeck, near Whitby, long before the First World War. A true story, George, and the hidden treacle tins full of sovereigns might still be there – in Littlebeck, that is, not under Rita Murphy's land!'

I then told George about Claude's deal with the chest of drawers and he smiled. 'Serves him right,' he said.

I went home for lunch and about an hour and a half later drove to Rita Murphy's home at Hollings Intake. An Intake, by the way, is a patch of moorland which at some time in the past has been enclosed then reclaimed as agricultural land. There are many examples throughout the North York Moors and they are usually named after the person who enclosed them. Thus there are Morgan Intake, Pearson Intake, Brown's Intake, Coates' Intake and, in this case, Hollings Intake. In the local manner of speech, this is sometimes shorted to Intak.

When I arrived, Claude Jeremiah was perched on his little rusting Ferguson tractor with Alfred sitting near his feet. He was hauling a plough through the soft earth and seemed very happy with his chore.

When he saw me approaching, he drew to a halt, but left the engine running as he came across to me. Rita Murphy also came out to meet me.

'Good afternoon, Claude,' I smiled as he came to a halt before me. 'You look busy?'

'Just helping out an old friend, aren't I, Rita?' he beamed, his eyes blinking at me. 'Neighbourly gesture, like, me being a friendly sort of chap.'

'Well, I do know Rita wanted her paddock ploughing, so I know your work is needed.'

She had arrived at my side too. 'It was so good of Mr Greengrass to offer,' she was genuinely surprised. 'And out of the goodness of his heart, too. He said he wants nothing from me.'

'Is that right, Claude?' I put to him, just to clarify the situation.

'Oh, aye, well, I thought she could do with a bit of help, Mr Rhea, and me having a plough I wasn't using, well, I thought it was neighbourly to turn the ground over for her ...'

'Well, I think that's very noble of you,' I said.

'Will you have a cup of tea, both of you?' she asked.

'Thanks, I would love one,' I accepted.

'Not for me,' said Claude. 'Work of this kind can't wait, you understand, strike while the iron's hot and all that ...'

And so I went indoors with Rita Murphy and she produced some lovely home-made scones, a pot of strawberry jam and two mugs of hot fresh tea.

'I can't understand why Mr Greengrass is so keen to plough my ground,' she said. 'He even offered to plant the potatoes.'

'Then let him,' I said. 'And when I come again I'll explain his generosity!'

And so Rita's small piece of Aidensfield was ploughed and planted by George Jeremiah Greengrass, and later she had a crop of beautiful new potatoes. Claude was given a sackful – but he never did find the treacle tins full of gold sovereigns.

Later in the pub, he asked me, 'Mr Rhea, that tale about those treacle tins of sovereigns. You didn't make it up, did you?'

'No, it's a true tale,' I said.

'Well, I ploughed all her land and found nowt,' he muttered.

'You might have to dig deeper next year!' I smiled.

3 By Chasing Two Hares, You'll Catch Neither

For duty, duty must be done,
The rule applies to everyone.
Sir W.G. Gilbert (1836–1911)

It was inevitable that our new sub-divisional inspector would attempt to impose his wisdom upon the rest of us. Such is the way of those new to the power of command. It seems that the police service, like any other profession, is riddled with new brooms which always want to make clean sweeps, even if the places in question have been swept clean times without number on many different occasions and in many different ways.

I am convinced that organizations like the police service, and especially departments of local authorities, keep their staff in work only because they regularly change their procedures, names or intended purposes. 'Reorganization' is the key word; in my time at Aidensfield, for example, the Civil Defence department was reorganized every two years simply because they had nothing else to do. There were very few civil people to defend! Eventually it was decided to rename it War Duties department, and as such it was reorganized even more frequently, chiefly because there were no wars to fight and thus no duties to perform. But the constant challenge of reorganization kept people in work and prevented boredom.

With the arrival of a new inspector, therefore, we felt it was inevitable that he would want to change something. Thus it was that Inspector Pollock called a meeting of all the constables of Ashfordly Section. Sergeant Blaketon was also instructed to attend. With bated breath we assembled in the muster room of Ashfordly Police Station, boots shining and hair neatly trimmed, to await his arrival and to find out what changes he intended to implement. Sharp at the appointed time, 10.30 one Thursday morning, he appeared before us like a vision – boots gleaming, trouser-seams and the front of his tunic sleeves pressed until they were like knife edges, not a fleck of dust anywhere and not a hair too long nor a whisker out of place. He stood before us, erect and stern, like a wax model of a supercop, but he was real.

'Good morning,' he said, and we duly chanted our reply.

'I am very concerned about the level of law-breaking in this sub-division,' were his first noble words. 'I know I have not been here very long but already I have been deeply disturbed by the unlawful behaviour of many local people and I have decided that we, all of us, should make a concerted effort to enforce the laws of this splendid England of ours. If law breaking becomes endemic, the whole of society will crumble,' he was in full flow now. 'The well-being of this nation has been built upon the willingness of the British people to accept the laws of the land, irrespective of class, colour and creed. We, as police officers, have been charged with the awesome responsibility of enforcing those laws, laws made by Parliament; I might add, the Mother of Parliaments. Our Parliament has set an example to the rest of the world. We should not shrink from our duty to enforce its laws.'

He paused for a moment, his eyes glistening and tiny beads of sweat appearing on his brow and cheeks. He was sensing greatness now, he was enjoying this; I got the impression he thought he was Winston Churchill stirring us into a fine and noble war effort. Then he continued,

'I have therefore conducted a detailed survey into law-breaking in this sub-division and have concluded that far too many motorists are parking without lights. Cyclists are even riding without lights during the hours of darkness. It is my intention, therefore, to conduct a campaign of effectiveness. With effect from today, each of you will endeavour to report for summons every motorist who parks without lights and every cyclist who rides without displaying obligatory lights to the front and rear of the machine. I have had a supply of special forms printed; I appreciate the difficulties of interviewing drivers who leave their cars upon the streets at night, but if you find a car without lights, you will place one of these forms upon the windscreen, directing the owner or driver to report to the nearest police station with his or her driving documents.

'They will then be interviewed by the office constable and reported for summons for whatever offences are disclosed. And this, you all know, is a fine way of checking driving licences, insurance, motor vehicle excise licences and details of vehicle registration. Many people forget to record changes of address or fail to sign their driving licence – all will be reported for process if offences are disclosed.'

It is fair to say that every man present groaned deeply within; we did not issue a loud, corporate groan, but suppressed our deepest feelings with honour. Every constable at that momentous meeting knew that this sort of purge had been done before, always with disastrous results. It seemed to be the aim of every new inspector to go around upsetting the local people. As things were, the local police used common sense when enforcing the traffic lighting regulations; we'd never dream of booking drivers who parked their vehicles unlit at night in cul-de-sacs or quiet back streets. If someone parked their unlit vehicle on a busy main road or in a dangerous position, then the law would be enforced, if only to teach the offending motorist a lesson in common sense. But to prosecute every driver who parked without lights, especially in remote rural areas, was sheer stupidity and it was guaranteed to alienate the public. In one quick burst of petty law enforcement, we could ruin years of good relations between police and public.

At that time, every motor vehicle parked on the streets during the hours of darkness had to show obligatory lights; these consisted of two white lights to the front and two red lights to the rear, with one of each for motor cycles and some other vehicles. The law applied to every public road in every town and village. Lorries, buses, cars, vans and motor cycles

were all expected to obey this law, the only exceptions being
tram-cars and vehicles used on railway lines. Furthermore,
even at that time, those lights had to be kept properly trimmed
(that was the actual word used), in a clean and efficient
condition and they had to be attached to the motor vehicle in
the prescribed manner.

There were special provisions for invalid carriages,
horse-drawn vehicles, pedal cycles with sidecars, horses with
or without riders, wheelbarrows, prams, hand-carts, lawn-
mowers, agricultural implements and lorries with overhanging
loads. If we were to enforce every law about the use of lights
when vehicles were on the road, we should be considered
persecutors who were operating a police state. But as
experienced officers, we knew that the finest way to show
Inspector Pollock the error of his ways was to obey his orders
meticulously. It was inevitable, therefore, that his scheme
should become known as Pollock's Purge. And there was no
finer person to obey those instructions to the letter than
Sergeant Blaketon.

One of the old school of police officers, he was the sort of
policeman who, if the inspector told him to jump off a cliff in
the course of his duty, would do so. Having served in the
army, Sergeant Blaketon would never question a lawful order.
After listening to the inspector's added views on how we
should go about our new law-enforcement duties, we left the
office to resume our normal patrols.

Alf Ventress was fuming with suppressed anger. 'This is
bloody ridiculous!' he snarled. 'I can see what's going to
happen – every night, you lot will stick notices on all vehicles
without lights and next morning, I'll be faced with a queue of
drivers a mile long as I check documents and report them ...
they'll all be blowing their tops ... I can see trouble brewing
but if that's what he wants, that's what he'll get.'

Alf was right. That night, the patrolling constables of
Ashfordly sub-division planted tickets on every car which was
parked without lights. I was off duty that night, so Aidensfield
escaped the first flush of Pollock's Purge, but as the night-duty
constables went off duty at 6.00 a.m. another day was
dawning.

And so it was that for hundreds of motorists the new working day began with the discovery on their windscreens of white pieces of paper headed 'North Riding Constabulary'; these were stuck beneath their wipers and exhorted them to pay a swift visit to Ashfordly police station, and to take along their licences and insurance.

At the station, they would be reported for summons for the offence of parking without lights. A lot of our customers would be late for work that morning and many would have stories to tell their colleagues. The police force would suffer yet another bout of canteen criticism – some victims' stories about being booked for parking without lights would make their experience seem more serious than having a hospital operation.

While a substantial proportion of the motorists of Ashfordly were trudging towards Alf Ventress and Ashfordly police station clutching their licences and insurances and at the same time wondering about the cost of a new battery for their cars, I was preparing for my morning patrol of Aidensfield. I had no intention of booking every motorist whom I discovered parking without lights – my relationship with the village people was too important to jeopardize for the sake of such a futile aspect of law enforcement – and so I decided to patrol the village and warn all the residents of the inspector's orders. Pollock's Purge would soon be hot news in Aidensfield.

Such warnings were generally appreciated. An old rural bobby once told me that the best way to ensure that people bought licences for their dogs was to walk into the post office and announce that you were going to inspect every dog licence in the village. With the speed of light, word of the constabulary intention would reach every dog owner in the district.

The effect would be that all those without licences would promptly rush to the post office to obtain the necessary document. Thus the legal purpose was achieved with the minimum of work by the police and also without the hassle of upsetting a host of forgetful dog owners.

I reckoned the same logic would work with car lights and so I paid a visit to all the key establishments in Aidensfield, such as the pub, the garage, the shops and the post office and issued warnings, in the strictest confidence, that the new inspector had ordered a purge on all cars parked without lights.

I reinforced my news with the fact that I would be patrolling Aidensfield that evening, during the hours of darkness, to plant tickets on every car I discovered on the streets without lights. It was the confidentiality of the information I was imparting which produced the greatest impact and word of the inspector's crackdown soon reached those parts of Aidensfield which I would not normally visit. I knew that, from tonight onwards (at least for a week or two), all cars would either be parked off the road or they would display the necessary lights. The village would be aglow; it would shine like Blackpool Illuminations.

With regard to the lack of car lights, I knew, as I began that first car lighting patrol, that visitors to the pub and to evening functions in the village hall were likely to be the worst offenders. I recalled from past experience that many people would enter the premises in daylight and forget about the car they'd left outside; as the sun sank in the west in Ashfordly, so the law would approach such cars with the intention of compiling yet another offence report. But that would not happen in Aidensfield. I detested that kind of impersonal approach – if the cars were likely to cause a danger, I would walk into the premises and ask the offending owners to switch on their lights. Many would do so without a quibble. Sometimes I would switch the lights on myself because most cars were never locked – there was no need to lock them because, at that time, most people were honest and did not steal from unlocked cars. It was a simple job to reach inside and operate a light switch.

And so, that first night, as I patrolled my village beat, sometimes switching on car lights and sometimes getting car owners out of their homes, the pub or the billiards match at the village hall to put on their lights, I realized that most parts of the village were rather like a major city. There were lights everywhere. I had never seen so many cars with their sidelights blazing and I made sure my uniform was seen as I patrolled the rows of parked vehicles. I felt that the campaign was something of a success – I had achieved this result without issuing a single ticket.

It was with some surprise, therefore, that I saw a small black car creep into the village and park outside the pub. The time was nearly ten o'clock and the car was displaying lights. As I approached, I realized it was the new inspector. I went closer, chanted 'Good evening, sir,' in a fairly loud voice and slung up a smart salute.

'Good evening, PC Rhea.' He climbed from the little vehicle, returned my salute and asked, 'Everything in order?'

'Yes, sir, all correct,' I chanted in the regulation tone. 'All cars correctly parked and illuminated. No cars parked without lights.'

'Yes, I have performed a tour of inspection around Aidensfield,' he said. 'And I must admit I am impressed by the law-abiding nature of the villagers. You clearly run a very efficient beat, Rhea.'

'Thank you, sir.'

I took him into the pub and introduced him to George; Pollock's eyes scanned the assembled locals who fell into a respectful silence as he scrutinized them, doubtless seeking under-age drinkers, but nothing untoward caught his eye. Even Claude Jeremiah Greengrass, sitting with a pint in his hands, made no comment.

'A very well run establishment, Mr Ward,' said Pollock. 'An example to many others, I would suggest. Well done.'

'We do our best,' beamed George. 'We have no wish to break the law here in Aidensfield, Inspector.'

'Thank you, Mr Ward,' and he left with me at his side. He then decided upon a short foot patrol of Aidensfield, to get acquainted with the layout of the village.

As we perambulated, we discussed a few local matters such as the crime rate for Aidensfield, the lack of any special constables in the village, the overall conduct of the other licensed premises on my patch at Elsinby and Crampton and, apparently satisfied, off he went, a happy man. When I was sure he'd driven out of Aidensfield, I returned to the pub to thank George for his co-operation; he'd ensured that all his customers were on their best behaviour tonight and so that first brush with Inspector Pollock's law enforcement strategy was over. But I knew he would return. I could not relax my vigilance just yet.

I learned afterwards that it was a different story in Ashfordly. Throughout that first day of Pollock's Purge, poor Alf Ventress had been faced with a queue of very irate and upset residents; they queued out into the street, they had all received tickets and all had presented themselves as required. The determined night-duty constables had visited every nook and cranny of the town and had swamped hundreds of unlit cars with tickets.

On the morning after the first phase of Pollock's Purge, poor old Alf had been at the receiving end of a non-stop tirade of verbal abuse and complaints; there were grumbles about a police state, about the insensitivity of the purge, about the daftness of having to display lights at the end of a no-through road and about the mentality of the police who sought to persecute motorists instead of solving real crimes.

A local magistrate, a doctor, two solicitors, several dozen holiday-makers and sundry other people had been caught. The catch included several moving vehicles whose lights had been faulty, several caravan units, a hand-cart, a lorry with a load projecting more than the specified distance without the specified lights, a mechanical crane, a yacht on board a low-loader, several pedal cycles without lights and a horse-drawn agricultural implement, namely a binder.

It was not a happy day for Alf; in addition to coping with the bad-tempered customers, he had problems explaining the law on the lighting of hand-carts more than two and a half feet wide by more than six feet long and four and a half feet high; the rules about tail lights on horses, white lights on motor-cycle sidecars and whether a combine harvester travelling backwards needed red and white lights at both ends. In short, it had been a downright miserable day for Alf.

It would not be a happy day for the court officer either; Sergeant Bairstow, the man whose task it was to get these offenders to Ashfordly Magistrate's Court, would have the chore of issuing summonses and bringing all these malefactors before the bench to answer the charges against them.

When Alf had finished his miserable spell of duty at five

o'clock that first day, his place had been taken by PC Alwyn Foxton and that evening he was faced with a continuing stream of angry motorists.

As Alwyn was to say later, he had no idea there were so many car drivers in Ashfordly. The night-duty shift had certainly been active and while Alwyn had been dealing with them in a most patient and apologetic manner, Inspector Pollock had arrived. Sergeant Blaketon had been in the office, too, helping to process the non-stop stream of offenders. As the new inspector had marched past the queue to gain access to the office, some had booed him, recognizing him as the architect of their misery. Alwyn had stood briefly to attention before continuing with his work and then Pollock had said, 'Ah, Sergeant Blaketon. Still on duty, eh? That's what I like to see, a man dedicated to the work in hand, a really conscientious officer ...'

As Blaketon had taken Pollock into his office for a discussion about the effectiveness of the purge, a large rotund man with jet black hair and dressed in a smart grey suit had entered the police station. He had pushed past the queue shouting, 'Where's that man Pollock?'

Before Alwyn could stop him, he had thrust his powerful way past everyone and had entered the police office, his face red with anger and his fists clenched.

'Just a moment, you can't come in here, this is private, please wait outside, sir, take your turn ...'

'Turn?' the man had blustered. 'I'll give him turn. Do you know who I am?'

'No, but that is the public area, out there, you are supposed to wait in the passage,' said Alwyn.

'I am Detective Superintendent Galvin, Regional Crime Squad and I want to see Inspector Pollock. Now.'

'He's with the sergeant, sir, through there ... I'll show you ...'

'No need, I can find my own way. Now, who are all these people? Why are they queuing like this?'

Alwyn had explained about Pollock's Purge whereupon Galvin had thrust his head through the hatch, 'Right, I'm overruling this foolish escapade. All of you, hand in your tickets and get away home. You'll not be prosecuted. This is ridiculous. And you, Constable, take those tickets and cancel them. And cancel any more who come in. Do it on my authority. I'm pulling rank on that bloody stupid man. And I'll get the sergeant to cancel those who have come in earlier. That man Pollock has just ruined weeks of carefully planned work by the Crime Squad, we've lost a major criminal through this stupidity and I'm going to have his guts for garters, so help me.'

And he stormed along the corridor towards Sergeant Blaketon's office.

'Very good, sir,' smiled Alwyn with some relief.

It was later that we learned the full story. The voice of the angry detective had carried into the office where Alwyn had suddenly found himself alone with a pile of useless tickets. But even as Alwyn carefully cancelled each ticket, more people were entering with their slips of paper. Alwyn simply warned them to display lights next time and sent them home.

He told us later, however, that Detective Superintendent Galvin had bellowed at the inspector, making him acutely aware of the fact that he had ruined a major crime squad exercise to trap a gang of important villains. It seemed that a group of northern criminals were planning a series of armed raids on building societies and crime intelligence had alerted the Regional Crime Squad. In the event of there being insufficient evidence to prosecute all the plotters when the actual raids occurred (the raids would use only two or three men out of a total of eight or nine plotters), the Crime Squad needed evidence sufficient to sustain a charge of conspiracy against them all. And they had learned that the group was to meet at a house in Ashfordly – on the very night of Pollock's Purge.

The CID, in several unmarked vehicles, had positioned themselves in various strategic places which provided a good view of the house and all who entered it that night. Night cameras, radio controls and an entire back-up team had been gathered for this operation, with the detectives concealed in vehicles disguised as a fruiterer's van, a plumber's van, a bread van, a caravan and car and sundry small private cars.

And at the crucial moment, as four of the suspects were walking towards the house, a uniformed constable had appeared.

The four suspects simply kept on walking, they did not even attempt to enter the drive of the target house; clearly they had seen the constable and had thought he was keeping observations. Thus, in that very simple way, the exercise was ruined and months of hard and even dangerous work had been rendered useless. And to add insult to injury, all the Crime Squad vehicles had received tickets for parking without lights, that being their means of merging unobtrusively with the other cars parked nearby.

Detective Superintendent Galvin was not a happy man and spent the next half-hour shouting his anger into the shell-like ears of Inspector Pollock. It did not appear to worry him that his verbal abuse could be heard by everyone in the police station, and probably everyone in the street outside. He was determined to embarrass Inspector Crispin Pollock.

Galvin's outburst had the desired effect. Next morning, the inspector issued an instruction which cancelled his campaign of effectiveness; we said somebody had pulled the plug on Pollock's Purge. But some good did result from his idea – for a very short while, the garages in Ashfordly and district did a roaring trade in new bulbs and 12-volt batteries.

*   *   *

It was the poet Matthew Green (1696–1737) who wrote that

> *Experience joined with common sense,*
> *To mortals is a providence.*

What is common sense to some, however, does not necessarily appear to be common sense to others. Some unfortunates don't have much common sense and there are others who lack any semblance of this most basic of human gifts – we can all quote examples, as do-it-yourself enthusiasts who bring down portions of their houses by stupid work, motorists who set off for a strange part of England without even a map in the car, picnickers who light fires on tinder-dry moors, people who work on electrical wiring without switching off the power, people who go sailing on the sea without any previous experience. Most of us can provide many other examples of sheer idiocy. Sadly, many of these silly actions result in extra and unwelcome work for Britain's police officers and I often think the police officer's job is to tidy up the mess that others leave behind. In some ways, police officers are the salvage operatives of a very careless society.

In trying to define common sense, most of us who suffered from Pollock's Purge considered it was something he lacked. Inspector Pollock was an academic, not a practical sort of character and it seemed he was going to go through his career making an almighty mess of most things. He seemed to possess lots of bizarre theories which could never work in practice. Furthermore, his lack of common sense was, unfortunately, compounded by a corresponding lack of experience in his job and we felt that this was not a very welcome combination in a senior officer of supervisory rank.

In spite of his shortcomings, however, we did feel he would learn from his experiences. But he did not. After getting lost in the woods at Aidensfield, and then the fiasco of his vehicle lighting purge, he decided he would organize a crackdown on local pubs.

The two aspects of pub life which upset him were those landlords who served under-age drinkers and those who did not close at the required time. After-hours drinking was a well known and very popular sport in most rural areas and most police officers tolerated this, unless it really got out of hand. Tolerance of the liquor licensing laws was one of those unwritten aspects of police work which need to be tempered with humanity, a precise understanding of the laws and, of course, common sense.

Quite a lot of us could not understand why one could sup from a pint of beer until precisely 10.30 p.m. while the same act was illegal only ten seconds later. Fortunately, that law was changed in the 1960s, allowing a ten-minute drinking-up time. But even so, the liquor licensing laws were fairly rigid. It must be stressed, however, that the police do not make the laws – that is done by Parliament and the task of the police is to enforce them without fear or favour, however daft some of them appear to be. And so Inspector Pollock, in his infinite wisdom, decided to enforce the law on the sale and supply of alcoholic drinks which were consumed after permitted hours. Under-age drinking could be tackled at a later date.

Now, most rural police officers know that a pint of beer supped after closing time tastes infinitely better than one purchased within licensing hours. It would not be breaking any confidences to report that many off-duty police officers have enjoyed a pint or two after hours. Furthermore, it would likewise be truthful to say that many of them were very senior officers. For policemen to find a pub which served drinks after hours was like finding an oasis in the desert; at the end of the permitted drinking hours the bar curtains were drawn, the doors locked and the assembled multitude got down to the serious task of supping their golden nectar. This act was somehow a defiance of the silliness of the liquor laws and there was a deep satisfaction in beating the system.

Police officers knew that once the awful shout of 'Time gentlemen please' rent the air, the beer assumed a delicacy of its very own; it became like ambrosia, the mythical food of the gods, a golden life-giving liquid which helped its supporters to get through the tough days and weeks ahead. And so men risked their reputations by drinking late. The landlord risked his licence by selling alcoholic drinks after time and those who were caught drinking risked public humiliation in the courts and in the local newspapers. Drinking late was as exciting as driving a racing car. It was a very risky business – but almost every pub was prepared to take that risk for the comfort and well-being of the customers. It was indeed a rare inn which closed exactly on time every night of the year.

Oddly enough, many town inns did close on time, chiefly to prevent trouble from some of their more robust customers, but in rural areas there were isolated hostelries in lofty places which were meccas for the faithful. Even if the law was being bent slightly, who could honestly claim that they suffered from the cheer which flowed from their study walls? There were few neighbours to complain and most of the imbibers did not have cars, preferring to walk home and so enjoy the still

night air of the moors. Some even sang to themselves during
the homeward journey, a sure sign of their ability to commune
with nature in the bliss and solitude of the calm night hours.

It seems that Inspector Pollock, a non-drinker, did not fully
appreciate these finer points. He lacked any hint of romance
and had never even tasted a glass of best bitter, his drinking
being restricted to a small sweet sherry at Christmas. Thus his
views were biased against the most English of pastimes.
Following his arrival at Strensford, we discovered that he had
undertaken several missions into the countryside specifically
to check up on late-opening inns.

Armed with a list of rustic hostelries, he had sallied forth in
his official car, and indeed had sometimes performed the
journey when he was off duty. He had toured the inns, noting
the names of those whose bar lights were still shining at eleven
o'clock or later, noting those with cars and bicycles parked
outside after closing time and writing down the names of those
with the noise of happy voices coming from within.

And he had been shocked by his findings – he discovered
that every moorland inn and village pub within Ashfordly
section was busy after closing time. Inspector Crispin Pollock
had therefore decided to have a second purge, this time on
village and moorland inns. It was to become known as
Pollock's Public House Purge.

It ought to be said that the period in question was one of
impending change for inns and public houses. In addition to
the ten-minute drinking-up concession, many were offering
bar snacks; some took advantage of changes in the licensing
laws to open smart restaurants and another factor was that
members of the female sex were now visiting pubs without the
risk of being labelled as women of doubtful virtue. To sit in
the lounge of a country inn and sip a gin and tonic was not
then considered quite as sinful as some might have suggested a
few years earlier.

It needs to be further added that the raiding of pubs whose
landlords sell drinks after licensing hours required the
extreme cunning and superb skills of those who used a wooden
horse to gain access to the ancient city of Troy. If landlords
decided to sell drinks after licensing hours, they did not leave

their doors open so that the police could enter the premises and catch them in the act. They locked the doors, closed the windows and drew the curtains to make the place secure against any raiders, whether they were police officers or late-night drinkers who'd been ejected from other places.

Acquiring the evidence necessary to gain a conviction was therefore very difficult but this did not deter the gallant Inspector Pollock. He gathered us together for lectures on the art of raiding pubs, reminding us that we needed evidence of the sale of alcohol, that we must catch the customers with the drinks actually in front of them and that we must seal every glass and initial it with a note of its contents.

Thus we would raid licensed premises armed with sticky labels and pens; the idea was to rush to a table of drinkers, order them not to move and then stick a label over the top of each glass saying, for example, 'Three-quarters of a pint of bitter seen before a man who gave the name of Eddie Donohue.' Logically, we had to obtain the names of the drinkers, take photographs of the scene if possible, seize all the evidence and warn the landlord or landlady of the impending prosecution. Lots of officers were needed to raid just one pub.

And so Pollock commenced his Public House Purge. What he had failed to realize was that all the landlords in the district were very aware that a new and very keen police inspector had arrived. They knew he was operating in the vicinity and they knew what he would do. Like generations of new inspectors before him, he would raid their premises and so they were prepared for whatever action he might take. Their response to a purge on after-hours drinking was very simple. All doors were locked at the end of licensing hours.

Those drinkers who were leaving would be told to simply let themselves out but make sure the latch dropped. If a police raiding party wanted to gain admission, therefore, they would have to knock or otherwise demolish the door. If they knocked, the landlord would alert the drinkers who would immediately dispose of their beer, either by drinking it quickly or pouring it down the sink. Thus by the time the police actually gained access to the bar, they would be confronted by lots of empty glasses and many happy customers playing dominoes or discussing horse racing, politics or some other topic, all of which were quite lawful.

Some police would gain entry by subterfuge, pretending to be a travelling doctor and shouting that they must use a telephone. They resorted to various devices in the hope that the doors would be opened; other officers adopted the technique of waiting for a departing drinker to leave the door open just long enough for a large police boot to be wedged between it and the jamb, and so they would sneak in. Some even attempted to 'plant' undercover cops among the drinkers but this never worked. A stranger in the bar was a real giveaway! In any case, all these tactics were known to the landlords; Pollock's raiding parties attempted various schemes, but all failed.

Over a period of some six months, his raiding parties entered about seventy moorland inns and local pubs without finding one which was breaking any of the licensing laws.

He did find lots of men playing dominoes, lots having earnest discussions about the government, the trades unions and the state of English football, but he never found anyone who was drinking after hours nor did he catch one landlord or bartender selling alcohol after time. And yet on every occasion that he passed those same inns whilst off duty at night, the lights would be burning, there would be the sound of happy voices from within with cars and bicycles parked outside. He knew they were taking advantage of him, he knew they would be drinking late and there seemed to be nothing he could do to stop them.

The only casualty of his campaign was Sergeant Blaketon; everyone blamed him for the upset caused by the raids. He got letters from the Licensed Victuallers Association, he got stopped in the street by drinkers and landlords to be quizzed about his actions, while some thwarted drinkers even wrote critical letters to the press, claiming that the freedom of the drinking man was under threat. Poor old Oscar began to realize that he had to find a way of halting the menace which was Inspector Pollock. For all his faults, Blaketon did not rigidly enforce the liquor licensing laws – he did use common sense.

Blaketon was feeling very sore about the whole enterprise when I was in Ashfordly Police Office one morning. Then

Pollock arrived. He caught Blaketon in a particularly black mood due to yet another abortive raid which had failed the previous evening.

'Sir,' began Blaketon. 'I think we should halt these pub raids.'

'Give them up, Sergeant? Why, might I ask?' There was a look of defiance on Pollock's youthful face.

'Because we're not having any success, sir, it's a waste of valuable time and a waste of manpower. It's getting us nowhere, not one pub has been found offending against the law.'

'Perhaps you feel this way because you are shouldering the blame for the raids?' smiled Pollock. 'You should not shrink from upholding the law, Sergeant, however unpleasant it may be.'

'I must say I am getting a certain amount of antagonistic feedback, sir,' grunted Blaketon. 'As the first man to enter the premises, the leader of my team as it were, I am thought responsible for the organizing of these raiding parties. I do get rude comments in the streets, and some landlords are refusing to donate any more prizes for our Christmas raffles.'

'Sergeant, you disappoint me,' said Pollock. 'You don't win wars by giving up when the first battle is lost. We shall continue. I shall pursue my policy until I am satisfied that every one of those licensed premises is operating within the law, not just upon one night or for one week, but permanently. And I have not yet reached that state of satisfaction. So I shall expect more late-night examinations of licensed premises in your next quarterly return.'

'As you say, sir,' sighed a weary Sergeant Blaketon.

Pollock continued, 'Now, I am here to examine your register of dog licence inspections, register of explosives stores and your lost and found property books. In your office please, Sergeant. Now.'

And so they disappeared into the inner sanctum which we called Sergeant Blaketon's office.

I must admit I felt sorry for Sergeant Blaketon; in spite of his approach to most aspects of police work, his relaxed attitude towards licensed premises, especially those within

Ashfordly section, meant we never had any problems with the landlords. There were very few reports of drunkenness, few occasions of fights or other trouble and all the landlords ran well-conducted premises, even if they did occasionally allow late-night drinking. Not once had we had a complaint from a member of the public about late-night drinking or the general conduct of any pub; Pollock was the only person to make a fuss about it and it seemed he was going to persist with his hard-headed notion of raiding the pubs until the landlords and the customers became heartily sick of our presence. It was no way to gain the respect and co-operation of the public; if something serious occurred, we relied on the co-operation of the public but this stupidity would serve only to alienate them. I knew Blaketon was seeking some means of stopping these raids.

We all realized that Pollock's lack of experience let him down in this matter; whenever a pub was causing real problems through late drinking, the simple remedy was to park a police car outside at closing time. Then, as the customers left, at whatever time, a uniformed constable would stop and test every car and ask every driver to take a test to see if he or she was fit to drive. It was a simple but effective way of showing we meant business – and it was a fine way to emptying a pub, even during licensed hours! If Pollock had wanted to gain control over the pubs, that's how it could have been done. Easily, with no hassle, no confrontations. Just a police car parked silently outside, waiting. But if Pollock was going to continue with his purge, he must be taught a lesson. The question was, how?

As we pondered the long term ill-effects of his actions, it was Sergeant Blaketon who told Pollock he had received some prior knowledge that there was to be a late-night drinking session at the Chequer Board Inn on Cockayne Moor. Cockayne Moor was a lofty area above Rannockdale and the inn was perhaps the most isolated of all those upon the moor. Once, long ago, a drovers' road passed this way and the ancient inn had served the drovers while their long lines of foot-sore cattle rested on their way from Scotland to York. Now, the inn was popular with hikers and tourists; it stood alone surrounded by nothing but open moor, the nearest house being five miles away. Few policemen ever raided the place and so it was a true haven for serious after-time drinkers. They came from far and wide to sample the fresh moorland air and the gorgeous golden bitter which had the flavour of heather within its bouquet. The Chequer Board Inn had a large clientele from Middlesbrough, Redcar and the smaller communities around Teesside. And it did not lie within Ashfordly section, therefore it was not the responsibility of Sergeant Blaketon and his officers. It did, however, stand within Strensford sub-division and it was consequently within the jurisdiction of Inspector Pollock.

I was working in Ashfordly police station one Saturday morning, completing a road accident report, when Sergeant Blaketon came through. He was smiling. I was surprised by this: he appeared to be in a very good mood.

'Listen to this conversation, Rhea,' he said. 'I need a witness. I am about to ring Inspector Pollock at Strensford.'

With no more ado he dialled Strensford police station on the internal network and said, 'Sergeant Blaketon here, put me through to Inspector Pollock, please.'

He waited as the connection was made and then I heard him say, 'Ah, good morning, sir. Blaketon here. Yes, all's correct. Now, my reason for ringing, sir. It concerns late-night drinking. I've received a tip-off, sir, from one of my informers. There is to be a late-night drinking session at the Chequer Board Inn; no, the licensee has not applied for an extension of hours nor has he notified us of a private party.'

Blaketon beamed at me as he made that call, adding, 'Well, sir, I cannot help, it's not within Ashfordly section, sir. It's just over my boundary. It's part of Challonford section. But I thought I had better pass along the information, should you wish to take action.'

And that was it.

Blaketon could see my puzzled expression and said, 'You heard me make that call, Rhea, eh? I was not secretive, it was all done openly.'

'Can I ask why I had to witness it?'

'I am hoping that Inspector Pollock raids that pub tonight,' he beamed. 'I want him to know that I passed the information to him openly and not in a conspiratorial manner.'

And with that, he returned to his office, chuckling to himself.

The whole story emerged later. The chief constable of one of the smaller police forces in the Midlands had rented a country cottage on the moors in order to celebrate his twenty-fifth wedding anniversary. Having been born and bred in the North York Moors, he had lots of friends and relations in the vicinity, including the chief constables of Middlesbrough, Durham, the North Riding of Yorkshire and Sunderland. All had been invited to a huge party at the Chequer Board Inn. There was a total of sixty guests, and dinner had been provided in the dining room. It was a good night, highly enjoyable and highly successful.

At midnight, Inspector Pollock and his party of two sergeants and eight constables were position around the isolated inn, waiting and watching. The place was humming with activity; the chink of coins could be heard as money was dropped into the till. Among the cars parked outside were two coaches and one overnight camper. The inn was ablaze with lights and full of people. Pollock realized that the men had to come outside to visit the toilet and had issued instructions that the raid would commence at 12.15 a.m. precisely because he had noted that the exit door was never locked. There was the point of entry.

He had no idea that inside were five chief constables, several local dignitaries, magistrates and county councillors as well as family members of those important guests.

At 12.15, Pollock gave the order. 'Enter the premises, immobilize all the drinkers, label each glass and specify its contents ... report the licensee for selling drinks after licensing hours and report all the drinkers for consuming intoxicating liquor otherwise than during licensing hours. Right, men. Go!'

This time, due to the certainty of his actions and the volume of customers present, he led the raiding party. Once inside, he shouted for attention; he ordered everyone to stop whatever they were doing and announced that this was a police raid. All

drinks would be seized as evidence. All names would be taken
… the licensee must not move!

A deathly hush had fallen as the army of police officers went
to work with Inspector Pollock leading the action, shouting
orders and demanding co-operation.

After watching him for a while, and after smiling as the
constables sniffed the drinks in an attempt to identify them, a
tall gentleman stood up and said,

'Inspector Pollock. I am your Chief Constable. And these
gentlemen here are also chief constables … now, I think this
little bit of fun can cease …'

Pollock was flustered, but only momentarily. 'Sir,' he said, 'I
received information that after-hours drinking was occurring
on these licensed premises and, in accordance with my
statutory powers, I have entered the premises to find everyone
drinking … sir, with due respect, the law applies to everyone
and if you and the other chief constables are found to be
drinking alcohol after the permitted hours, I shall have no
alternative but to report this matter.'

At this, there was loud applause from the party. It seemed
they all thought this was a stunt performed as entertainment for
the guests but the Chief Constable raised his hands for silence
and said, 'Inspector, we are celebrating the twenty-fifth
wedding anniversary of Mr John Lodge, the Chief Constable of
Stamfordshire. As you may know, he holds a senior post within
the Salvation Army and he does not drink alcohol. It is a
condition of any social gathering which he arranges that no one
drinks alcohol. We are all drinking non-alcoholic drinks.'

The expression on Pollock's face changed from one of
authority to one of doubt; he looked around. His sergeants and
constables, one by one, said, 'This is orange, sir …' 'This is
bitter lemon …' 'This is lemonade …'

The Chief Constable went on, 'And as we are not drinking
alcohol, we are not committing any offence. There is no law to
say we cannot remain on licensed premises after hours, and
there is no law which says the landlord cannot sell soft drinks
after hours. Therefore, there was no requirement to apply for
an extension of hours, nor was there any need to notify the local
police of a private party.'

And at that, the entire party erupted into cheers and Inspector Pollock slunk out of the pub, followed by his smiling constables. He drove away without saying a word.

And that marked the end of Pollock's Public House Purge.

4   *Poetic Justice*

'Twas a thief said the last kind word to Christ;
Christ took the kindness and forgave the thief.
Robert Browning (1812–1889)

Among the many very interesting houses on my beat was one
called Poets' Corner. It occupied a splendid riverside site at
Crampton where its well kept lawns and gardens sloped gently
to the edge of the water. At the bottom of the garden, among
some thick reeds, there was a small pier which jutted into the
water where the family, called Eastwood, maintained a tiny
rowing boat which they used for trips along the river. The
boat was always moored near this jetty and I often thought its
open aspect was a security risk. A burglar could easily row his
own boat to this point, raid the house from the rear, and
escape with his loot without anyone seeing or hearing him.
And yet the house had never, to my knowledge, suffered such
an attack.

The house itself, a fine Georgian structure of dark moorland
stone with a blue slate roof, stood at the top of the garden,
with more lawns separating it from the road which twisted and
turned through the picturesque village. The main windows
overlooked the river with spectacular views across the dale
beyond.

It was a house that appealed to all who had had the good
fortune to visit it and the Eastwoods were regarded as friendly
and welcoming people. There were two large entrance gates
which opened on to the road; these led into the garden and
then into a parking area in front of the house. There was lots
of space before the house and the garden was occasionally

open to the public for charitable purposes, such as raising money for the Red Cross or for the repair of the church roof. Thus a lot of people had visited the gardens, which were beautifully maintained and full of interesting shrubs, flowers and rock plants.

Its chief attraction, however, was the unique collection of statues of famous British poets. Mrs Judith Eastwood, a lady in her mid sixties, was widely known as a collector of such statues – over the years she had scoured salerooms, antique shops and cottage sales in her search for these statues and her collection was now regarded as the finest in Britain. Indeed, it was perhaps the only one in Britain and included some items in wood or stone; others were fashioned from a type of plaster like the statues found in many Catholic homes. One or two were even made from glass, some of them solid, others hollow. Other materials included marble, Whitby jet, brass and even concrete!

Several were very large, almost the size of human beings, while others were of a more modest size, perhaps standing two to three feet tall. Some were a mere eighteen inches high.

She had some miniatures too, these being only six inches in height. These were kept indoors, as were all the most valuable or fragile examples. Some of her statues were several centuries old, such as a wooden one of Shakespeare. The larger ones, particularly those made of stone and some of the wooden ones, stood out of doors and occupied prominent positions about the garden. During the winter months the wooden ones would be taken into an outbuilding to avoid the weather, but in summer all the more robust examples reappeared in the garden to stand like silent sentinels, surveying all before them.

I don't think Mrs Eastwood knew precisely how many statues she owned; there were umpteen Shakespeares in stone, wood, glass and plaster, countless Miltons and Bacons, several Cowpers, Swifts, Tennysons, Wordsworths, Shelleys and John Donnes and miscellaneous minor ones such as Walter Pope and Sir Thomas Wyatt. She claimed that every British poet of note, born before 1900, was represented and her knowledge of British poets was such that few doubters had the expertise to challenge her claims. It would have been a nigh impossible task to discover which were missing.

It was this collection which brought visitors to her garden on its occasional open days; in addition, various poetry societies and parties of aficionados from the poetry world would enjoy private visits by appointment. With such a diverse crowd of visitors, I must admit that I worried about the security of her statues.

I had no idea of their individual monetary value since there did not seem to be a large market for such statues – I knew of no other collector who would want to steal them. But one Monday morning in late June Mrs Eastwood rang me. Someone had stolen a wooden statue of Geoffrey Chaucer.

I drove to the house and my first task was to examine the scene of the crime. Mrs Eastwood, a tall, very slender and rather handsome woman with dark, greying hair, led me into the garden along a maze of paths. Eventually we halted beside a bed of roses. There was an empty stone plinth on top of a small, ornamental dry stone wall.

'He was there,' she pointed to the empty place. 'He was standing right there last night, I checked. And now he's gone, Mr Rhea.'

'You've searched the garden?' I asked. 'Sheds, outhouses, places where it might have been hidden?'

'Everywhere. My husband and I searched every single hiding place, including the reeds beside the river, the boat and the compost heap at the far end of the garden. He's gone.'

I was intrigued by the way she referred to the statue as 'he', almost as if she was referring to a real person, and, after conducting my own search of the area for clues such as footprints left by the thief, I began to note the necessary details. One factor to consider was whether Geoffrey could be quite easily carried away by one moderately strong person.

Fortunately Mrs Eastwood had several colour photographs of this Geoffrey; I was able to borrow one which I would be able to reproduce and circulate via police channels to antique dealers and others to whom the statue might be offered for sale. She explained that the statue was some two feet six inches tall, carved from dark oak and clothed in Chaucer's period, the fourteenth century. Carved on the foot of the statue, upon the base where the feet were resting, was the outline of a large church, probably Canterbury Cathedral. The statue depicted Chaucer as a sharp-featured man in late middle age, sporting a white goatee beard and white hair; it was based on the portrait used by Thomas Occleve in his *De Regimine Principum*. The artist was unknown.

Mrs Eastwood was uncertain of the age of the statue, but informed me that experts had dated the wood and the style of carving as the middle seventeenth century. She reckoned it was worth about £250, but that was a very arbitrary figure. It might be worth far more to a serious collector. I then asked whether in recent weeks she'd had any suspicious visitors.

'The gardens were open yesterday,' she acknowledged. 'We had almost a thousand people looking around, for the Red Cross, and one man did ask if he could borrow that very statue.'

'Borrow it? What on earth for?'

'I have no idea, I didn't ask and he didn't explain. It was such an unusual request that I immediately turned it down.'

'Did he persist in his request? Was he a nuisance?'

'No, not at all; when I refused him, he apologized for troubling me and just wandered off to look at the others. I kept an eye on him, of course; I was worried he might be tempted to take one of my poets, but he didn't. I lost sight of him eventually and he never returned.'

'Can you describe him?' This man seemed to be a suspect, at least someone who ought to be eliminated as soon as possible.

Mrs Eastwood told me that the man was very distinctive in appearance. He had long and very scruffy dark brown hair which came down almost to his waist; he wore casual clothes – jeans and a multi-coloured shirt 'rather like those one was accustomed to seeing upon Canadian lumberjacks,' she added. He had sandals on his feet but wore no socks, and he sported a long, unkempt beard which was the same colour as his hair. She said it was difficult to estimate his age but she guessed he'd be in his late thirties or early forties, although she might be years out due to his hirsute appearance. When I quizzed her about his mode of speech, she said he was well-spoken without any discernible accent; he did not wear spectacles and she did notice that his teeth were in very good condition.

She had no idea how he'd arrived at the open day, whether he rode a bicycle or had come by car; he did not appear to have any companion and other than his asking her if he could borrow Chaucer, she'd had no contact with him.

At that time, it was fashionable among young people, especially those of artistic temperament, to live in so-called hippie communes. Regarded by many as gentle and caring people, hippies sought an alternative society which was free from the constraints of authority and tradition. They wanted to be free to live their lives as they wished. Some became known as flower people but, sadly, they did attract the more unsavoury elements from the baser levels of our society.

Drugs, promiscuity and widespread irresponsibility became associated with some of these communes, which were being utilized by those who had, in their own words, 'dropped out' of society. These drop-outs were dirty, dishonest and even violent, the very opposite of the original notion of the gentle flower people. So hippie communes began to attract an unsavoury reputation. It was sad that these well-meaning groups drew the worst elements of society into their midst; the result was that no self-respecting village or town wanted a hippie commune within its boundaries or even within a reasonable distance. One or two hippies did venture into Aidensfield and district, but they seldom remained very long. After living for a while in derelict farms or old barns, they moved on, often leaving rubbish and damage in their wake. In spite of their gentle image, the hippies' hangers-on earned them a bad reputation. Having listened to Mrs Eastwood's description of the man at the open day, I did wonder if another hippie commune had developed in the vicinity.

Her description of the visitor had all the hallmarks of the kind of person who would frequent such places and the odd request to borrow Geoffrey Chaucer was the kind of behaviour one might expect from them. I could imagine a commune of hippies sitting around a camp fire reading aloud from his *Canterbury Tales* and thinking that the life of the pilgrims somehow mirrored their own existence.

Having extracted all the necessary details needed to compile my official crime report, I set about my enquiries, beginning in Crampton. It was a compact village on the southern slopes of the dale and, like so many communities in that area, boasted a peer of the realm, a shop, a post office but no pub. This was because Lord Crampton did not wish to attract unsavoury characters to his village – and he did own most of the property. Several breweries had offered to purchase or rent suitable premises as an inn, but he constantly refused.

I started by asking Stuart Cannon, owner of the village shop, whether he had seen this character around the place and his response was immediate and positive.

'Yes, Nick. Regularly. Once a week he comes in here to buy provisions – fruit and vegetables, groceries, a magazine or two – the usual stuff any householder might purchase.'

'Who is he?' I asked.

'No idea,' he spread his hands in a gesture of defeat. 'He just comes on Thursday mornings, gets his stuff, pays in cash, and leaves. He doesn't seem to want to get into conversation.'

'Is he new to the village?' was my next question.

'Well, he's not a native,' Stuart told me. 'I should think he's around for the best part of a year or so. I never ask about his private life and he never volunteers anything.'

'Where's he live?' I asked.

'I wish I knew. So far as I know, he's not using one of the houses in Crampton. He just appears, always on foot, buys his provisions and disappears. He carries them in a rucksack on his back. I did hear he's been seen walking along the road towards Ploatby but when he leaves me he usually goes into the post office.'

When I realized I could get no further information from Stuart, I pottered across the road to the post office, which was run by Dorothy and Laurence Porteus. I explained the purpose of my visit and Dorothy smiled,

'It sounds like Mr Chatterton,' she said. 'He comes in here once a week to collect his mail. He uses us as an accommodation address. Garth Owen Chatterton is his name, we get quite a lot of letters for him, addressed care of this post office. He has a post office savings account with us too, he pays money in and draws it out from time to time.'

'Where does he live?' I asked.

'I don't know, he's never told us. I just assumed he lived somewhere nearby. He's been coming in to see us for about a year now, always on Thursday. Shall I tell him you wish to speak to him?'

'No, that might frighten him off!' I laughed. 'I'll try to arrange my duties so I'm in Crampton on Thursday. What's his usual time of arrival?'

'Mid-morning,' she said. 'He's not in any trouble, is he?'

'Not to my knowledge,' I told her. 'But I do need to have a word with him.'

And so I left the post office, knowing that news of my interest in this character would soon filter through the population. At least I had made some progress and it only remained to find out where the mysterious Garth Owen Chatterton was living. If the village post office had no idea, then Crampton estate office might be able to help. That was my next visit. But the secretary to the estate manager said that none of the estate's cottages or properties was occupied by a Mr Chatterton. They did have one or two vacant premises which were available for rent, but he had never expressed any interest.

Before returning home for lunch, I did encounter one or two other residents of Crampton as they went about their daily business. In each case, I approached them and asked if they had encountered the mysterious long-haired Mr Chatterton. The only one who could help was a young married woman called Rose Harvey. She explained that sometimes she drove from Crampton to visit her mother in Aidensfield. Usually she made the trip on Thursdays and had sometimes noticed the long-haired man walking along the road which led to Ploatby. Sometimes she'd seen him heading towards Crampton; at other times he'd been heading in the opposite direction. The description she provided made me positive it was the same man but, like the others, she had no idea where he lived.

After lunch, I checked the electoral registers for each of the villages on my beat, but none contained the name of Chatterton. Likewise, I checked with CID at Force

Headquarters to see if the name had cropped up in our criminal records, but it had not. I realized I had a mystery man living on my beat. But where was his home? And what was his interest in Mrs Eastwood's statue of Geoffrey Chaucer?

As I went about my duties that Monday afternoon, and throughout the following Tuesday, I made enquiries in Aidensfield, Elsinby and several of the other tiny communities that formed my beat. But no one had seen Chatterton in those villages. Then on Wednesday, as luck would have it, I encountered Claude Jeremiah Greengrass as he was walking to the pub for his lunch-time pint. I decided to quiz him about the missing statue, not seriously thinking that he was the culprit but rather as a matter of routine. I quizzed him about every crime that happened on my patch – it was part of our on-going professional relationship.

'Morning, Claude,' I greeted him. 'Nice day.'

'It was till you showed up,' he grunted.

'So where were you on Sunday night?'

'In bed, where I should be, that's where. Why? Has somebody been nicking pheasants?'

'No, statues.'

'Statues? What sort of statues? And why would I pinch a statue?'

'To sell it and make a bit of cash.' I then decided to switch my line of questioning to confuse him. 'So who's this long-haired chap that's wandering about?'

'You're baffling me now, first asking about statues and then a long-haired chap. Are you accusing me of something?'

'You?' I laughed. 'Why should I accuse such a fine, upstanding member of the community of anything? No, Claude, I am endeavouring to solve a crime. Somebody has stolen a fine statue of Geoffrey Chaucer from a garden in Crampton and a long-haired, untidy specimen of a man is suspected.'

'Well, I'm well-dressed, neat and tidy, as you know, so it can't be me.'

'So who is this long-haired untidy chap? Fortyish, waist-length hair, scruffy, walks everywhere ...'

'It'll be that chap in Elsinby Forest,' Claude said, trying to get himself absolved from whatever suspicions I had. 'Lives in that old lumberjacks' hut, deep in the forest. Mind, I'm not saying he took the statue! I'm no grass! And he does walk everywhere ... I've seen him ... when I've been walking ...'

'When you've been poaching, you mean!'

'You blokes are never grateful for us citizens helping you with your enquiries. You'd think I'd learn a lesson and keep my mouth shut ...'

'The only reason you're helping me is to get yourself off the hook so I'll stop asking you awkward questions, but your help is appreciated. So come into the pub, I'll buy you a pint,' I heard myself offering. 'That'll help you realize I do appreciate your help. Then I must be off.'

In the bar, I surprised the landlord, George Ward, by buying a pint of beer for Claude, but none for myself as I was in uniform and on duty. I remained a few minutes for a chat, asking Claude to describe the old huts. Eventually, I realized where they were. Deep in Elsinby Forest, which comprised rows and rows of conifers planted some forty years earlier, there was a complex of disused huts. They were far too deep within the trees for a casual visitor to discover and they had been used by forestry workers when the plantation had been first prepared; for a time, they'd used the huts as they nurtured the young conifers but over the last twenty or thirty years the complex had been deserted. I had never had any reason for visiting the buildings, and in fact they were so deep within the forest that they were almost impossible to locate. But now I had a reason for finding them.

I went to see Harry Bolton, a retired forestry worker who lived near the church and, with the aid of my own map of the area, he told me how to locate the huts.

'We built 'em when we were planting that forest, way back in the twenties,' he said. 'Good sturdy huts, there's toilets even, with running water collected from a beck, a canteen, bedrooms. You could live there ... we built 'em strong, we knew they'd be used when the trees were harvested, that'll be any time now, I shouldn't be surprised. They'll be usable still, Mr Rhea, dry and warm.'

He explained how to find a route through the endless rows of pines, so that afternoon I set off in my minivan. Once inside the forest, I followed the old tracks, taking note of my route when I turned left or right, and sometimes marking trees with large bows tied from a length of orange tape I carried. It was so easy to get lost in the featureless world of tall tree trunks and when I reached a stream to which Harry had referred, I parked the van and walked.

In total, it took me nearly an hour and a quarter to find the huts, but eventually I did see them through the trees, a small complex of wooden chalets with log walls and felted roofs. All were in first class condition. But as I approached, I heard noises. I could not identify the sound at first, but it did sound like someone chipping at a piece of wood with a chisel. And as I entered the enclosed area before the huts, I saw a long-haired man sitting on an old tree trunk as he chiselled at a block of ash wood before him. I saw him long before he saw me; and there, on a table in front of him, stood Geoffrey Chaucer.

I stood and watched him for a few minutes; he was totally unaware of my uniformed presence as he concentrated upon the work in hand. I could see he was carving a wooden statue; he was, in fact, copying Geoffrey Chaucer, making a smaller version of Mrs Eastwood's famous poet. After observing him for some three or four minutes, I decided, with some reluctance, that I must break his concentration.

I walked into the area and hailed him.

'Mr Chatterton?'

He looked up from his work with never a sign of anger or fear on his face; through all that hair he smiled and said, 'You've come for Geoffrey?'

'I have,' I said. 'I'm PC Rhea from Aidensfield, I've had a complaint that you stole the statue ...'

'Borrowed, Constable, borrowed. I'm not a thief. I borrow statues to copy them, that's all. The lady at the house would not consent to my borrowing of this one, so I helped myself. I shall return Geoffrey to his plinth when I have finished with him.'

'So what are you doing with him?' I had to ask the question.

'I am copying him. I am a sculptor, Constable, and I

specialize in the British poets. I have never yet found a statue of Chaucer, not until this Sunday, and so I have never produced what I believe is a passable image of him. And then I found this Chaucer – at a house just down the dale.'

'So you took him?'

'I borrowed him. I asked the lady, who refused – not surprising, judging by my appearance, but appearance isn't everything. I saw the advert for the open day when I was in the post office last week and, well, her having all those poets in her garden, and me specializing in carving poets …'

I looked at some of his work which stood on ledges in what used to be the former canteen and felt sure Mrs Eastwood had bought some. They did look distinctly familiar.

'Where do you sell them?' I asked him.

'Wherever I can, craft shops in York, market stalls in Ashfordly, shops in Malton and Scarborough, London even, or the Lake District. Wordsworth and Coleridge sell very well over there …'

'But you must not help yourself to other people's goods,' I said. 'That's larceny.'

'I'm sure she'd have given me permission if I'd been allowed to explain myself,' he said. 'She has a lot of my statues in her garden, that big one of Milton is one of mine, I had to copy that. There aren't many Miltons about, you know … I always return them when I've finished.'

Had I proceeded by the rule book, I should have arrested him, seized the statue of Chaucer as evidence, and taken him to Ashfordly Police Station to be charged with larceny. That was then the word for theft.

But equally, I knew the law. For the crime of larceny to be committed there had to be an intention by the thief at the time of removing the property to permanently deprive the owner of the property. That criminal intention was lacking in this case. Unauthorized borrowing was not a criminal offence, except in the case of motor vehicles for which special laws had been made. Any court of law would throw out this case, I felt sure. But I could not let the matter rest – after all, I had received a complaint of a crime and I had found the person responsible for removing the statue.

'Are you going to arrest me?' he said, his smile flashing in the dim light of the forest.

'No, but I am going to ask you to accompany me to Mrs Eastwood's house,' I said. 'I want you to bring Geoffrey Chaucer with you, and some other smaller examples of your work, just to prove that you are what you say you are. You and Mrs Eastwood have a lot in common. And when she meets you, I think she will withdraw her complaint about the stolen statue.'

'You're a gentleman,' he said. 'Well, no time like the present. Come on, I'll put a few smaller poets in my haversack ...'

I helped him to pack a selection of his work, and then we journeyed to see Mrs Eastwood with me helping him to carry the burden. As I'd expected, she was astonished, partly because she had indeed been buying his work without realizing he lived and worked nearby.

She was clearly delighted that she now had Geoffrey Chaucer back home. I then explained the law on theft. When I finished, she said, 'Mr Rhea, I could not possibly prosecute this man, not now. Besides, as you have explained, there was no crime, was there? But just think, if I hadn't reported it, I would never have met Mr Chatterton ...'

Thus I would be able to write off the incident as 'No Crime'. As she showed the scruffy sculptor around her amazing collection I realized that here were two kindred spirits. She made us a cup of tea and produced some home-made cakes, and as we talked it was clear that Mrs Eastwood was happy to permit Chatterton to make use of her own superb collection of poets. And so he would be able to widen the scope of his work as he borrowed some of her rarest examples.

'Tell me,' she said as they grew more absorbed in their conversation. 'Are you by any chance related to Thomas Chatterton?'

'Yes,' he said. 'I'm from that family, although he died in 1770, aged only seventeen. Even in that short time, he had earned a fine reputation as a poet. That's how my interest in sculpting poets arose.'

'And one of my ancestors was Thomas Love Peacock,' she smiled. 'He died in 1866, and that's how my interest in poets arose ...'

The time had come for me to leave and I rose to my feet. 'I will run you back to the forest,' I offered to Chatterton.

'No, allow me, Mr Rhea,' begged Mrs Eastwood. 'I do so want to see Mr Chatterton's other work and he can, of course, keep Geoffrey until he has completed his work.'

And so the saga of Poets' Corner was over. I rang Sergeant Blaketon to inform him of the outcome and he said, 'I suppose it's poetic justice, Rhea. Did you know that Geoffrey Chaucer was the first poet to be buried in Poets' Corner at Westminster Abbey?'

'No, Sergeant,' I said. 'But all poets steal from Homer, so they say.'

'So long as they don't steal from Mrs Eastwood, I couldn't care less,' he grunted.

* * *

Another problem of dishonesty arose when the Aidensfield coal merchant, a man with the very apt name of Tony Hopper, came to report that small amounts were being stolen from his depot. He ran his business from the goods yard of the railway station and at that time the stocks of coal and coke were not locked away. Anyone could help themselves and, as a new arrival in Aidensfield, I found this general open trust somewhat unusual. Upon my very first visit to meet Tony, I expressed my doubts about this quaint system, but he assured me that there was no need to lock away the coal or coke – no one ever stole from his stocks. The people of Aidensfield could be trusted, he said. And, as things turned out, that was true.

In thinking about the availability of the coal and coke, it would have needed a wheelbarrow or a vehicle to carry away a sufficient amount to be useful, although the odd lump could be pocketed or carried off by hand. And if anyone did set about stealing from the depot, even at night-time, then surely the villagers would see them at work with their barrows or sacks and inform Tony. And so the coal and coke bays remained open to everyone, and yet none was stolen.

That was until Tony Hopper began to realize his stocks were dwindling, albeit by small amounts. He began to suspect something was amiss when he found evidence which suggested that someone had swept up some loose pieces in one of the bays, so he began to mark the extent of the spread of each of the six bays of coal. Small pebbles, discreetly positioned, showed him the extent of the coal as he finished work each evening. And then, next morning, he saw that at regular intervals a small amount had vanished – enough to half fill the average coal bag on each occasion, in his estimation. The unthinkable was happening – someone was stealing his coal.

He maintained his own system of checking stocks for a few days before involving the police. And when he called at my police house, I could see he was far from happy.

'If it's somebody who's hard up, they could have it for nowt if they asked,' he said. 'Damn it, Mr Rhea, I'll never see folks short, especially in winter. But to sneak down to my depot at night and steal, well, it's a miserable thing to do.'

There is no doubt that this betrayal of trust was hurtful to him, but after checking that no one had been given any authority to remove the coal I decided to 'crime' it, as we say. That meant that the disappearance of the coal was formally logged as a crime and not written off as mere wastage, which in turn meant I had to keep observations and make enquiries about the losses. It also meant that my colleagues from Ashfordly would keep observations during their patrols of the district. Upon learning of these crimes, Sergeant Blaketon laid scorn upon Hopper's method of storage.

'The man's a fool, Rhea,' he grumbled. 'You don't leave valuable materials lying about so that thieves can help themselves. He's asking for trouble ... serves him right. I'll bet he's been losing coal for years without realizing ...'

'No, he hasn't, Sergeant. That's the whole point, it's never been locked away, never been placed behind locked gates or in locked yards; for years it has been stored at the railway station in all six bays of that open-fronted depot.'

'CID will think we're idiots, criming this one,' he muttered. 'How much has gone? Do we know?'

'No, Sergeant, not exactly, there's no way of telling.'

'Well, what I'm asking, Rhea, is whether there is one crime or several. If this has been happening once a week for the past six, sixteen or twenty-six weeks, that's a separate crime on each occasion, and that will play havoc with our statistics. All those unsolved crimes ...'

'It'll be nice if we catch the villain, though,' I beamed. 'We'll be able to write off a lot of crimes as "detected".'

'That's *if* you catch the villain, Rhea! And that is something I feel is highly unlikely! These sneak thieves are the very worst.'

His attitude made me determined to arrest this sneak thief but Blaketon was right in saying that the arrest of this kind of villain was never easy. The thief was not coming to the depot on the same evening each week, for example, and we had no idea of his hour of arrival. It was fairly certain, however, that he came during the night, probably in the early hours, say around two or three in the morning when no one was around. He must have had a vehicle of some kind to carry away his ill-gotten gains, however, so I decided to keep observations whenever I was engaged upon a night patrol. It was a hit-and-miss method, but as I had many other duties to occupy me, I could not afford to spend every night sitting in a coal yard just in case the thief turned up.

Over the next three months I spent many lonely hours hiding in different sections of the railway complex of buildings, listening for sounds of illicit shovelling and watching for people lurking in the shadows armed with shovels and sacks, but, on those nights, no one came. He did arrive several times when I was not there! I began to wonder if the thief knew when I was concealed in his happy hunting ground, but felt not – no one knew. I hadn't even told Tony Hopper or the railway station staff of my intentions. And then I struck lucky.

It was a chilly night in November with a full moon and there was also a thin covering of snow on the ground. It had fallen since midnight and now lay like a virgin white sheet across the landscape. Its presence combined with the light of the moon added a glow to the area, highlighting the heaps of coal, the buildings and the roads in and out of the station. And, in the silence of that night I heard noises near the coal depot. I did not move; I was sitting in the waiting room with the door open (it was never locked at Aidensfield station in those days) and listened as the sounds continued. From this point, every tiny noise in the station could be heard and I guessed no one could steal coal without making some noise.

I also knew that if I was to prove a case of larceny, I would have to catch the thief with the coal in his or her possession – catching him or her in the act of moving towards the supplies was not sufficient. So I waited, ears straining to catch every hint of noise and to identify the sounds. And then, clearly, in spite of the distance between my hiding place and the bays, I could hear the sounds of someone shovelling coal. It was a most distinctive noise and it echoed in the confines of the bay under attack.

On silent sponge-rubber soles and armed with a torch I padded along the platform and down the short track which led towards the coal bays.

The trip took about thirty seconds with my dark uniform effectively hiding my movements within the shadows of the surrounding buildings and trees in spite of the brightness of the night. I left a trail of footprints in the snow and as I approached the bays I could see the distinctive wheelmarks of a pedal cycle in the thin snow on the road surface. The marks headed straight for the depot and vanished somewhere within. Most important of course, was the fact that there was only one track – it meant chummy had arrived but that he had not yet departed; indeed, I could still hear the scraping sounds from within. He was at work. I knew from the noise that he was filling a bag with coal; I knew I had caught the thief.

Guided by the wheel marks in the snow, I crept around the edge of a protruding wall, my boots making not a sound, and now the noise was louder. In the gloom of the bay in which he was working, I could see the occasional flash of the blade of the shovel as I caught glimpses of his white face and a half full sack standing a pool of dim light cast by the front lamp of his cycle. He was using its light by which to work.

I waited for a moment, taking in the scene; the cycle stood

against the wall of the bay, its lamp fixed low on one of the front forks, the front wheel angled so that the light shone upon his area of operation. I could see the shadowy figure hard at work, his breath forming clouds of vapour on the cool night air. I had no idea who it was, however, except that it looked like a smallish male person.

Having seen all that I wanted, I suddenly switched on my torch to brightly illuminate the man and shouted, 'Police, don't move ... stay right where you are ... drop that shovel ...'

I had to make him drop the shovel; it could have been used as a weapon against me, but with a sharp intake of breath, a sign of shock and surprise, he obeyed. The shovel crashed to the concrete floor of the bay and I was surprised to see the man raise his hands in the air. I approached him with caution, kicked the shovel aside and told him to place his hands behind his back. He obeyed. Quickly, I snapped on my handcuffs; even so, there was always a risk that a person arrested in these circumstances would attempt to make a dash for freedom, but this man did not.

Meekly and with apparent signs of resignation, he submitted to the arrest and said, 'Sorry for doing this, Mr Rhea ...' Now I recognized him; he was a small, middle-aged man called Dennis Brooks who lived in the council houses with his widowed, invalid mother. I escorted him to my van, sat him in the passenger seat and then drove around to collect the bag of stolen coal and his bike. I squeezed both into the rear of the little van and drove to Ashfordly police station.

Sergeant Bairstow was on night duty and we submitted the meek little man to his fate. He was charged with stealing the coal and we kept his cycle and the half-filled bag as evidence; he was bailed to appear at Ashfordly Magistrates' Court on a date to be notified.

I then drove him back to Aidensfield. During the journey he did nothing but apologize; his actions were certainly out of character for he was a man who never went out drinking, who rarely took part in village events and who seemed to spend most of his time caring for his invalid mother. He'd lost his job as a delivery man with the Co-op and told me he'd been desperate. His mother needed warmth during the winter months and the coal fire was her only means of heating the house; they'd literally spent all their meagre savings on keeping her warm. In desperation he'd resorted to stealing coal to keep her as healthy as possible. Her pension managed to keep them in food but little else. I advised him to tell that story to the court; I felt sure that, in the circumstances, the magistrates would be lenient when imposing sentence upon him. I dropped him at his home and said I would be in touch with him about the date of his court appearance.

Having not got to bed until 4 a.m. I walked to the coal depot the following lunchtime to inform Tony Hopper of the night's developments. He was delighted, but when I identified the culprit, his expression turned to one of sorrow.

'Not poor old Dennis!' he said.

'Why, you've had dealings with him?'

'Aye, he got behind with his payments, I let him have several loads on tick, Mr Rhea, saying he could pay when he got some money in. Well, he never paid, so I stopped delivering his weekly order.'

'He needs the coal for his mother, she needs constant warmth but now he's out of work,' I told Tony. 'He's lost his job with the Co-op.'

'Has he? Poor little devil, he never said! If he'd told me that, I'd have given him the bloody coal! Why didn't he ask instead of just helping himself ... folks are daft, Mr Rhea, putting themselves at risk for the sake of asking. Too proud to ask for charity, but daft enough to risk being arrested.'

'I've told him to explain all this when he goes to court, Tony,' I said. 'I know they'll treat him with compassion.'

'If I'd known he was out of work, I'd have offered him a job,' he said. 'I need a spare man at the depot, to do a bit of bagging up and delivering. None of the young lads wants that sort of heavy work, so I'll see what he says. If he's willing, I'll set him on.'

'Are you sure?'

'Aye, 'course I am. And I'll tell the court what I've done, that'll mebbe get him off with a caution or summat similar, conditional discharge mebbe.'

And that very same day, Tony Hopper went to visit Dennis

Brooks to offer him a job. Dennis accepted with tears in his eyes and within a week I saw him bagging coal at the depot and occasionally driving the delivery wagon around the villages. When Dennis appeared at Ashfordly Magistrates' Court, Tony came along to speak in his defence and proved an eloquent and persuasive witness.

The outcome was that Dennis was given a conditional discharge for stealing coal, the condition being that he did not commit any further offences of a like nature within the next two years.

'I won't,' he promised the court. 'I'll be able to keep mother cosy and warm in winter now because I get free coal. That's one of the perks of my new job. I am allowed as much free coal as I need.'

5   Give a Dog a Bad Name

A good dog, like a good candidate, cannot be of a bad colour.
Peter Beckford (1740–1811)

One of the things that intrigues me is the manner in which a craze will suddenly arise, become popular, and then fade into obscurity. There are times when one wonders what prompted the craze to begin in the first place and why so many normally sane people so slavishly followed it.

My favourite, as I have mentioned on previous occasions, is the Alexandra Limp. During the 1860s, Queen Alexandra, who was then the Princess of Wales, had a minor accident as a result of which she developed a very slight limp. For some weird reason, it then became fashionable for many of the ladies of her time to walk with similar slight limps. This peculiar whim became known as the Alexandra Limp. But why on earth would anyone want to copy someone else's limp? I'm sure Her Royal Highness thought those people were all rather strange.

Similar things happen in the fashion world, such as hair styles, types of shoes, female facial adornments, short skirts, flared trousers or variations in collars and ties, while in other spheres crazes like hula hoops, yo-yos and executive toys seem to come and go with remarkable speed. The world of fashion depends upon people who follow such changes.

None the less, I continue to find it odd that people will surrender to these whims, only to abandon them within a short time. It seems such a waste of money and effort. A lot of men, of course, studiously ignore fashions, having learned that the suit they bought as a lad will be acceptable for many years to come. After all, it really doesn't matter what one wears, so long as one is comfortable.

As I am writing these notes (in 1993), the mobile telephone is the latest fashionable craze but whether it is a rich person's plaything or genuinely useful has not yet been determined. It might merely be part of another fashion.

I cannot understand why some people feel they must emulate others – I can think of all the Elvis Presleys who continue to haunt the world, all the Marilyn Monroes and all those who consider themselves a double of someone famous. Why not be themselves instead of copying another person? I think there is something faintly sad about those who feel compelled to copy other people or who doggedly follow trends which are set by others.

Such a phenomenon burst upon the scene in Aidensfield when Mrs Mildred Prenty of Frankland House bought herself a pair of Afghan hounds. Hers were a beautiful pair of animals, both bitches. They had rich, fawn, silky coats which were worn long around the ears, limbs, feet and hindquarters. These beautiful dogs loped along the village street in a most glamorous and elegant manner.

Their long, slender faces, curly tails and cheerful, gentle nature made them exceedingly popular with all who came into contact with them. There is no doubt they were very nice dogs; extremely well cared for, obedient, lovable and beautiful, they were a credit to Mrs Prenty.

But because Mrs Prenty was one of the most highly respected of social leaders in the neighbourhood, other ladies from Aidensfield and the surrounding villages decided to acquire Afghan hounds. In a very short time, the moors and dales seemed to be full of Afghan hounds in a variety of shades and colours, ranging from cream to fawn to red, brown and even black. For the social climbers of Aidensfield it became very trendy to own a pair of Afghans, and the dogs, with their owners at the end of expensive leashes, would promenade around the village for all to admire.

Some ladies, however, did not wish to be regarded as copiers of fashion; they saw themselves as leaders, and for this reason: they had to do something different. They felt they should not be owners of Afghan hounds. They could not think of anything drastically different which had the same social impact and connotations, so they all decided that ownership of some other kind of distinctive breed of dog was quite acceptable. As a consequence, some bought borzois, others settled for red setters while labradors, golden retrievers and collies were also strongly favoured.

There is little doubt, however, that the Afghan hound owners, being the originals, considered themselves the most superior. Their dogs seemed to think so too – certainly Mrs Prenty's dogs had an air of superiority and so did she. The outcome of all this social manoeuvring was that the Aidensfield and District Afghan Hound Owners' Association was formed, the idea being to organize club meetings, sometimes with talks from experts on matters like grooming and breeding with the climax of the year being the annual Aidensfield and District Afghan Hound Show. The Prenty Challenge Cup would be awarded to the best dog of the year; in prestige, it would be something akin to a miniature Crufts.

The non-Afghan-owning ladies, however, not to be outdone, decided to form their own societies, associations and clubs, each with their own shows and thus there were formed the Aidensfield and District Borzoi Association and Show, and similar associations and shows for labradors, golden retrievers, spaniels and collies, the last named scoring Brownie points by having an obedience section. There was even an association and show for Yorkshire terriers and another for Rhodesian ridgebacks.

One interesting factor about the Aidensfield and District Afghan Hound Owners' Association, however, was that their dogs were all females. Every one was a bitch, a fact which was said to echo the general feeling about some of their owners.

No one outside the Association was quite sure why this all-female trend had developed and various theories were propounded. although nothing on the matter was ever publicly stated by the owners of the lady dogs, it was generally felt that their owners' delicate upbringing in a ladylike society might not have enabled them to cope with boisterous and randy male dogs. As things were, these devoted ladies could mollycoddle their female dogs as if they were daughters;

most of the other villagers reckoned the bitches were more amenable to control than any daughters might have been.

Another factor was, of course, that if all the dogs belonging to the Afghan Association were female, then it would be highly unlikely that any of them would accidentally become pregnant by dogs owned by fellow club members. The owners could freely show off their bitches without rude attention from sex-mad dogs. Their virtue was thus safeguarded, their figures would never be distorted and the ugly question of suckling pups would not arise. Harmony and discretion would reign.

Being the village constable, I heard about these new dog clubs and was quite surprised that the Afghan Association was restricted to only female owners and to female dogs. The other dog clubs were open to male members and to male dogs, but the Aidensfield and District Afghan Hound Owners' Association was adamant. No randy male dogs would be allowed at the association meetings or at the annual show, and thus the risk of unwanted canine pregnancies would be avoided. It was the sort of logic one might expect from feminists, being their idea of equality and common sense.

In some ways, their caution was understandable because lots of other lady dogs in Aidensfield had had unfortunate experiences with a highly sexed and very determined masculine dog called Alfred. Alfred, the Lothario of the local canine world, lived with Claude Jeremiah Greengrass on the outskirts of the village and had an awesome ability to woo in spite of the most determined attempts to stop him. Whenever a bitch was in season anywhere in the area, Alfred would leave the comfort of the Greengrass establishment to fulfil his heart's desire as many times as he could muster before he was caught. He would travel miles to complete his lustful urges, being known to leap five-bar gates, cross snow-bound moors and wade through treacherous rivers to bring a little love and romance to his lack-lustre existence. As a result of Alfred's promiscuous roaming, lots of little Alfreds had been whelped in Aidensfield, sometimes to the considerable surprise of their owners, who'd been expecting something looking more like a cocker spaniel, a hare hound or a pedigree Alsatian.

Alfred's achievements had resulted from his ability to

capitalize upon the skills he had acquired in poaching for his worthy master; he was able to circumnavigate most attempts to frustrate his urges. After achieving the purpose for which he had risked life and limb, he would then leave the scene of his triumph with a happy smile upon his hairy grey face.

Lots of strange-looking pups had resulted from these activities and many a show-dog had had her reputation of purity ruined by the ardent Alfred. If there was a female dog on heat anywhere within Aidensfield and district, the lustful lurcher would seek her out and release his pent-up passion in a most vigorous, and sometimes spectacular, manner.

When the Aidensfield and District Afghan Hound Owners' Association decided to hold its first annual show, therefore, the organizers were mindful of Alfred's reputation and decided that the event demanded top-quality security measures. No one was quite sure whether or not the village hall defences were capable of thwarting Alfred in his most determined mood.

I was quite surprised, therefore, when they asked me for my recommendations. I was summoned to a meeting between Mrs Mildred Prenty, Chairman of the Association, and two ladies called Leonora Haddock and Ermintrude Appleyard. They had been elected to form a sub-committee with special responsibilities for the good conduct of the show. Over tea and cucumber sandwiches, while wedged between two silky-coated lady Afghan hounds, I listened to their worries.

Eventually, I said, 'Ladies, I cannot see any problem. Alfred will only pursue lady dogs when they are in season, and the answer would seem to be that all bitches on heat are therefore disallowed. They must be forbidden to enter the hall while the show is in progress. That would eliminate all your problems.'

'But Mr Rhea, you do not understand,' simpered Miss Haddock. 'All the dogs on show will be bitches, there will be no male dogs in the show and so the rule about bitches in season should not be necessary.'

'From my own rather limited experience,' I countered. 'I am led to believe that it is one of the courtesies, if not a specific rule in some cases, that bitches in season are not entered for any dog shows. The responsibility rests first with the owners, surely, and then with the adjudicators.'

'In mixed shows, that is understandable,' beamed Mrs Prenty. 'But I see no problem with an all-female entry. This is why we are seeking your advice. We need to keep all male dogs out of the hall during the afternoon of the show.'

'Clearly, a notice to that effect would be enough,' I tried to play down their concern. 'Most dog owners would oblige if they knew the reason – but can't I persuade you to disallow all bitches in season?'

'No, that is not among the rules of our Association,' said Mrs Prenty. 'That is why we are an all-female association; we want equality with those owners who show male dogs. We cannot and will not accept that females are different.'

'Then you need a good authoritative person on the door of the hall,' I suggested. 'And you are fortunate in that Aidensfield village hall does have a foyer; by keeping the inner door closed while coping with arrivals, you could regulate the entry of visitors – and dogs.'

'I think we could do with two door persons,' beamed Mrs Prenty. 'One to staff the outer door and one to control the inner one, with strict instructions to contain every incomer in the foyer until satisfied he or she is not smuggling in a male dog.'

'Absolutely right!' I said.

'Then will you be doorman?' smiled Mrs Prenty.

'It depends whether or not I'm on duty,' I said. I had no wish to become doorman to this gathering but when she gave me the date, I checked my diary and found I would indeed be on duty from 2 p.m. to 10 p.m. that Saturday afternoon.

'Sorry,' I said. 'I can't oblige, but I shall be on duty that afternoon and will make sure I visit the hall as regularly as I can.'

As I left them to their deliberations, I wasn't sure about the sense of allowing bitches in season to partake in a dog show, even one restricted to bitches, but it was their problem, not mine. As the weeks ticked by, I could see that the proud owners were giving their bitches the very best of beauty treatment. The most outstanding was undoubtedly a beautiful

and silky bitch called Jacquanetta. She was owned by Leonora
Haddock and was clearly the favourite to take the Afghan of
the Show award.

On the day of the show, a Saturday in late July, I walked
across to the village hall to find that the security arrangements
were in operation.

Large signs outside the hall, equally large ones on the
internal doors and a forbidding lady in tweeds, called Olga
Pitkin, standing at the main entrance, were suitable deterrents
to any masculine dogs. I did see several dogs hanging around
outside the hall, however; there'd be a dozen or more and
among them was a Yorkshire terrier, a Jack Russell terrier, a
Scottie, two whippets and a Pyrenean mountain dog. All were
scenting the air and getting restless. The lady on the door kept
shooing them away, sometimes resorting to a shepherd's crook
to propel them from the entrance.

I went over to her. 'You've not got a bitch in season in
there, have you?'

'Well, actually, yes, Mr Rhea. Three or four, in fact ... you
see, Mrs Haddock's Jacquanetta is such a lovely dog and we
know she has come in season, only yesterday in fact, and we
dare not ban her, being Mrs Haddock's bitch. And if she was
allowed in, then we could not ban the others who were in
season ...'

'So you've got several bitches on heat in there? There's no
wonder half the dog population is gathering outside! You'll
have to keep these doors firmly closed,' I said. 'If any of those
lustful dogs get half a chance, they'll be in there.'

'I know, that's why I am here,' she beamed. 'None shall
pass, Mr Rhea, I know how to deal with randy males!'

There was no answer to that remark, and so I left her to her
guard duties.

I undertook a patrol around the village, advising on car
parking, checking that car owners locked their doors against
thieves and generally making sure things were in order. It was
a nice gentle way of spending a couple of hours on a Saturday
afternoon. At least, that was my view until I saw the familiar
unkempt shape of Alfred the lurcher loping along behind a
hedgerow. His master was not with him; I could see no sign of

Claude Jeremiah and wondered why Alfred was skulking along the hedge in that furtive manner. But then, of course, everything he did was furtive; whatever Alfred did was usually devious, troublesome or illegal. Judging by the urgency of his manner, I felt sure he was heading for the village hall to attempt to partake in a spot of doggy courting, but in this instance he had a lot of competition. There were some very fit and aggressive dogs waiting on the green. Alfred would be unaware that this pack of lovesick hounds had already gathered; furthermore, he would never get past Miss Pitkin, her shepherd's crook and her system of closed doors. I was confident that the security network would defeat Alfred.

But I was wrong.

Unbeknown to anyone, Alfred had not attempted to enter the village hall via the obvious route. He had probably observed the crowd of panting dogs outside and had surely seen Olga Pitkin and her stick as she defended the front door. Being a cunning dog, he must have realized that all attempts to enter via the main door would fail.

With considerable intelligence, therefore, he sneaked around to the back of the hall. In a small room at the back the tea ladies were busy; the electric boilers were heating the water, the ladies had prepared all the cups and saucers, they had put bread and cakes on plates and were ready to distribute the teas. At a given signal, the MC would announce that teas could be purchased at the hatch, these ladies would then transfer their carefully prepared products to the point of sale. It was very hot work in the kitchen, what with the crowd of hard-pressed ladies and the steam that rose from the boilers. One of the ladies had opened a sash window, raising the bottom portion some three inches and lowering the top portion about a foot to produce a circulation of cool air.

Had anyone kept an eye on that window, they would have seen the distinctive grey snout of a lurcher as it sniffed the air through the open portion at the bottom. As the ladies set about selling their wares Alfred pushed his head through the gap, easing the window higher as he struggled to gain entry; eventually, he succeeded in pushing the window high enough to admit the whole of his body. He crawled through like a snake, writhing until he was able to drop the eighteen inches or so on to the floor of the tea room. From there it was but the work of a moment to sneak into the main body of the hall, where all the lady dogs were displaying their charms.

From eye witness accounts which later circulated the village, it seems that Alfred succeeded in keeping his presence concealed from everyone during his critical journey across the floor of the hall. He did this chiefly by sneaking under display tables and chairs until he arrived at the stand upon which Jacquanetta was displayed. Acting with the speed of a poacher's trained companion, he launched himself at Jacquanetta with all the skill necessary to achieve his purpose. Before any human being realized what was happening Alfred was locked in close embrace with his sweetheart. The moment he was sighted, however, there was pandemonium. Women screamed, chairs were knocked over, cups and saucers rattled to the floor, stands were overturned and sticks were discovered as a horde of angry women began to chase Alfred. He disentangled himself from Jacquanetta in a manner which brought tears to his eyes, and once again using his poaching skills managed to conceal his movements beneath chairs, tables, stalls, female legs and long dresses. Miss Pitkin, armed with her crook, sallied forth into battle as guardian of the show, and the chase began in earnest.

But when Miss Pitkin left her vigil on the doorway, all those other dogs which had waited so patiently outside saw their opportunity and rushed into the mêlée. There was a lot of barking and snarling, a lot of dog-fighting and a lot of love-making as Aidensfield village hall turned into a canine battlefield.

I heard the commotion and went to investigate, but as I entered I realized the entire show was an utter shambles and several women had been reduced to tears. It looked as if a whirlwind had gusted through the premises, destroying all before it and reducing highly bred dogs to quivering lumps of hairy flesh. And as I strode among the turmoil of dogs, people and village hall furnishings, I saw the distinctive figure of Alfred sneaking at a fast pace towards the tea room. I followed, thinking he was using the opportunity to steal some food.

But I was in time to see him disappear through the open

window, albeit with a ham sandwich in his jaws, and I realized how he had breached the security systems of the Aidensfield and District Afghan Hound Owners' Association to wreck their annual show. That was the first and last dog show to be organized by the Association, but some months afterwards a lot of strange-looking pups appeared on the streets. None could really be called handsome or of show quality.

Not surprisingly, there were several Alfred look-alikes among them. Alfred had had his day.

★   ★   ★

The Afghan/Alfred incident, as it became known, did concentrate the minds of those who wished to show their dogs. The ladies who had insisted on bringing their in-season bitches to the show were constantly reminded of their folly; their social pride had backfired upon them and no one was sorry.

But others began to argue that if in-season bitches were not allowed at the shows, there was no point in having an all-female entry. Male dogs could and should be allowed to compete. This then led to the other associations asking about the logic of having several such clubs, all paying separate fees for the hire of the hall, separate fees for speakers, separate bills for printing posters or the expense of organizing separate association events. If one of the clubs hired an expert to talk about dog hygiene, then the topic would surely be of interest to all the clubs. There were very few topics which were of interest only to owners of specific breeds. The outcome of several informal discussions led everyone to believe that it made financial sense to incorporate all the associations and to have one show for all members' dogs, irrespective of breed or sex. Numbers would be greater, costs would be shared and more opportunities would be created.

This led to a meeting of the committees of all the doggy associations in Aidensfield and the outcome was a decision to scrap all the individual clubs and to form one society as a replacement. While it was appreciated that most of the members would be dog owners whose desire was to breed and show their specimens to the world, it was also pointed out that many village people did own dogs which were not, and never would be, show material. There was a large number of mongrels in Aidensfield, most of whom were loved by their owners and it was felt they should also be allowed to join the society. They might enjoy and benefit from talks by experts; they'd learn from demonstrations about grooming, health and general welfare. Admitting 'ordinary' dog owners did present problems so far as the name of the new organization was concerned but after a great deal of argument it was declared that it should be known as 'The Aidensfield and District Dog Lovers' Society'.

It was felt that this name highlighted the love that existed between man and his so-called best friend and it included anyone who felt that the club would be of benefit to them and their pets. The outcome was a huge surge in membership – lots of country people kept dogs of one kind or another but few had access to expert advice about the training or care of their pets and so the new club became very popular.

One of the most ardent members was Claude Jeremiah Greengrass who felt that the lessons in canine control and behaviour, hygiene, welfare and treatment for illnesses would be of great benefit to his Alfred. As time went on, it became clear that Alfred was a highly intelligent animal, often knowing how to sneak away from the class to steal a piece of sandwich or how never to lie down or sit when instructed. Claude could make him obey, but few others possessed the knack. This was a device taught to their dogs by poachers so that no one could catch them when they were 'working' – indeed, some old poachers taught their dogs to come to heel by the command 'go away', and to leave the area by saying 'here, boy, here'.

Thus if anyone saw a poacher's dog at work and ordered it to 'come here boy', it would immediately run away. The order 'go away' or 'go home', would result in the dog coming to the heel of its master. It was part of a cunning system to ensure that no poacher's dog was ever caught by a gamekeeper, police officer or landowner. By the time of my spell of duty at Aidensfield, this ruse had been discovered and so most poachers had ceased to make use of it. None the less, poachers' dogs were still notoriously difficult to catch.

There was a great deal of interest in the dog training aspect and I was asked if the police-dog handlers would come to show how their Alsatians were trained. They readily agreed; their skills were appreciated and it was this kind of expert advice that made the new dog lovers' club both popular and successful.

It was inevitable that the club decided to stage its own dog show. This time it would be open to all dogs whether male or female, and whether of pedigree birth or not. There were classes for various breeds, classes for pups, classes for toy dogs, working dogs, sheep dogs and a whole host of others, with the inevitable 'best dog of the show' contest. The organizers, having learned from the Afghan/Alfred fiasco, did make a good job of the arrangements and, most certainly, no bitches would be admitted if they were in season. A state of calm should therefore prevail.

One of the classes was for the 'Best Working Dog' and as I examined the list of entries, I was surprised to see that Claude Jeremiah Greengrass had entered Alfred. There were no classes for lurchers, some purists refusing to recognize them as being a pure breed, and so this class seemed to provide an opportunity for Claude to show off his best friend.

The dogs had to be presented to the judges by no later than noon that Saturday; the dogs would be walked before the judges, examined and adjudicated upon before 2.30 p.m., after which time the public would be admitted. Members of the public would be able to tour the dogs on exhibition and witness further categories, such as the obedience section and the final walking of those dogs that had been placed on the short list for the best of breed, best in category and best in the show.

I decided to pay a visit to the show, purely out of interest. As I walked towards the main door just after the public had been admitted I was surprised to see Claude Jeremiah Greengrass galloping out with a look of absolute distress and misery on his face.

'Claude!' I knew something awful had happened. 'Claude, what's wrong?'

'Wrong? Alfred's been stolen, Mr Rhea. That's what's

wrong. Gone, he has. Spirited away. You can't trust anybody these days!'

'You're mistaken,' I said. 'If you left him there to be judged, he'll be with one of the officials, surely?'

'He's not, I've checked. Nobody's seen him, he's been spirited away, that's always a risk with valuable animals. Alfred is a rare dog, you know, Mr Rhea, the only one of his kind in these parts …'

I had to check his complaint, and when I entered the hall it was busy with members of the public and proud dog owners. Some exhibitors had rosettes pinned to their cubicles, and others were awaiting the final judging sessions, but when Claude took me to a section marked 'Miscellaneous Working Dogs' there was no sign of Alfred. There was a hook at the back of his stall, and I knew he would have been attached to that by either a chain or a lead.

'He was there, Mr Rhea, he was chained to that hook, sitting as good as gold when I left him, not making a fuss.'

'Was he a winner, did he get on the short list?' I asked.

'No, there's no other lurcher in the show, Mr Rhea, so he's a winner without coming here … no, he's been nicked. I asked that chap over there,' and he pointed to one of the stewards, 'but he said he has no idea where Alfred's gone.'

I approached the steward, who couldn't help; he'd come on duty at two o'clock, and said that Alfred had been absent at that time. I decided I had to make enquiries from the show secretary, for I had no wish to log this as a crime if there was some other explanation. Knowing Alfred, he'd probably sneaked off upon some doubtful enterprise, but it did mean someone must have released him from the securing hook in his stall.

The show secretary, Major Kennedy, was very helpful, checking all his judges' returns until he said, 'Well, Mr Rhea, Alfred was in his allotted position at five minutes to one. That's when Mr Evans, the working dogs judge, assessed him.'

'Did he win?' beamed Claude.

'No, sorry, Mr Greengrass. The record just says – "examined, no award made".'

'Aye, well, I expect yon judge'll be coming back to have

another look, mebbe he went off to bring a second opinion feller, Alfred's quality was mebbe that good that no one judge could believe his eyes. So where is he?'

'Well, Mr Evans has gone for his lunch, and I had mine at one o'clock, but must admit I never saw anyone remove your dog.'

It was far from easy making enquiries with Claude Jeremiah always trailing behind me, but by a process of elimination of officials it seemed that no one had seen Alfred leave the hall, either alone or with another person. I did learn, however, that the last person to have seen Alfred in his stall was Philip Crawford, a veterinary surgeon who lived in Aidensfield. He had a practice at Strensford, but often volunteered to help with Aidensfield events – on this occasion he was the show vet.

There was nothing in the secretary's files to show what the outcome of Crawford's inspection had been but I did detect a certain caution in Major Kennedy's demeanour. I felt sure he was withholding some information, but I failed in my efforts to gain any more from him. The only thing I did learn was that Mr Crawford had gone home for lunch. He was expected to return within half an hour or so. I said I would wait.

'Why would a vet want to see my Alfred?' asked Claude.

'He examines all the dogs in the show,' said Major Kennedy. 'We hire him to ensure that all dogs are fit to be here, his job is to check for illness, injuries, diseases and so forth, anything that might render a dog unsuitable for show purposes.'

Kennedy looked at me with steady eyes, almost as if willing me to remove the troublesome Claude, but Claude hadn't finished.

'Well, there was nowt wrong with my Alfred. Anyroad, I can't hang about here doing nothing,' he grumbled, and I could see the relief in Kennedy's eyes. 'My Alfred's gone and he could be anywhere out here, lying hurt ...'

'I'm sure he has come to no harm,' said Kennedy reassuringly.

'What about your house?' I suggested. 'Has he returned there? If he slipped his lead, he might have gone home. I know he often goes out alone and always returns to base by himself. He knows his way back to your house, doesn't he?'

'Shall I go and have a look?'

'I think that's a good idea,' I suggested, with the distinct feeling that Kennedy wanted to be rid of Claude.

I was delighted when he said he'd drive his old pick-up to the smallholding to check for signs of Alfred. I said I would remain here to continue my enquiries. With Claude out of the way, Major Kennedy relaxed.

I asked him, 'Is there something I should know, Major Kennedy?'

'Just that Claude's dog hasn't been stolen,' he whispered almost conspiratorially. 'Please keep this incident in low profile, Mr Rhea, we do not want a fuss, especially among the other exhibitors. May I suggest you visit Mr Crawford while Claude is absent? And depending upon what he tells you, may I then ask for the utmost discretion?'

'Yes, of course.' I was puzzled by this attitude and wondered what grave secrets lay with Alfred the lurcher. I decided that if the show secretary did not wish to tell me, then the answer must lie with Philip Crawford. Crawford lived in a large detached house on the outskirts of Aidensfield but within a ten-minute walk, and so I left the hall to visit him. He was just finishing his lunch as I knocked on his door and he invited me to have a coffee with him. I accepted.

'I'm here about the lurcher that was removed from the show,' I began. 'Claude Jeremiah Greengrass's dog.'

'The infamous Alfred,' smiled the vet. 'Yes, he's here in a kennel in my back yard. He's locked in, Mr Rhea.'

'A prisoner? Can I ask why?'

'He's covered with fleas, Mr Rhea, he's a walking flea pit. He should never have been allowed into that hall among the other dogs. So I removed him quietly, led him out of the back door and across the fields to my house. A small sub-committee, convened within a couple of minutes, decided we should not inform the other exhibitors, that the matter should remain secret. If any of them had known about this flea carrier, most of them would have withdrawn their dogs in the fear they'd become infected with the Greengrass flea strain. Some of those owners have spent hours grooming their dogs and some have spent a fortune on shampoos and beauty treatment. It would be awful if they became alarmed about Alfred's fleas. So it was a case of discretion being a better solution than valour. I smuggled him out of the show before anyone knew what had happened. I'm sorry if I caused you extra work, but he's in one of my kennels now, smothered in flea powder.'

'So he stays here until the show is over?'

'Yes, under house arrest, as you might say. I'll release him when the show's over.'

'OK, I agree. I'll get back to the hall and tell Claude we haven't located him yet. It might be best to spread the tale that he appears to have run away – perhaps his discarded lead might lend strength to that tale?'

Crawford smiled, gave me the old leather lead and I returned to the show. And so, to ensure that the show continued without disruption or alarm, I said I had found the lead lying in the long grass near the hall's south-facing wall. When Claude returned, I showed it to him.

'He's escaped, Claude,' I said. 'He's run off. The vet saw him when he examined him, he has to examine all the competitors and he was in the hall at that time.'

'He wasn't at home when I got there. I'll skin him alive if he's been up to summat!' snarled Claude.

And so the Aidensfield and District Dog Show concluded without any alarm; prizes were won, honours were achieved and the general opinion was that it had been a well-conducted and successful event. But as the dogs left with their proud owners, I did notice that several were scratching themselves rather vigorously. I said nothing.

Claude's Alfred would end the day without any fleas, thanks to a caring vet and a liberal coating of powder, but the legacy of his show appearance was that several other dogs had been infected. I knew of no criminal offence with which to threaten Claude, but I would be careful how I patted Alfred in the future. Later that night I rang Claude.

'Has your Alfred turned up, Claude?' I asked.

'Aye, he's back, Mr Rhea,' said Claude. 'I don't know where the hell he's been, but he's covered in powder and smells like a hospital sick bay.'

6   *On With the Dance*

Love's but a dance.
Henry Austin Dobson (1840–1921)

One of the more pleasant aspects of working as a rural constable was that there were few real trouble spots on one's patch. Problem places like night-clubs, football grounds and city centre pubs were unknown in villages like Aidensfield, Crampton and Elsinby; fights, mayhem and senseless violence were virtually non-existent. I must admit I was delighted with my work in such a peaceful haven, but we rural bobbies did have compassion for our town-working colleagues. They had to contend nightly with fights and disturbances in the vicinity of such places while we enjoyed a calm and contented way of life.

Even so, trouble could arise in rural areas. The two places most likely to attract it were the village pub and the village hall when dances were in progress. Fortunately, the landlords on my patch all kept their pubs in good order, often quelling trouble before it started, and it was very rare for the police to be called to a disturbance at any rural inn.

When dances were held at the village hall, however, they did seem to attract an unruly element. At one stage, weekly dances were held in Aidensfield village hall, but the ensuing trouble and vandalism quickly brought these dances to an end.

The weekly dances had ended just before my arrival; I recall my predecessor telling of one awful night when all the huge windows of the hall were put out by vandals during a bout of drunken stupidity. But that sort of violence was rare. The usual kind of bother consisted of punch-ups between rival gangs of youths. A gang would arrive from Thirsk with the sole intention of setting about another gang from Malton, with Aidensfield as their battle ground. There was no reason for these fights, other than the fact that the Thirsk lot disliked the Malton lot. And vice versa, of course. So the happiness of the dances was ruined, a sad thing for those who came for a good fun-filled time free from such idiocy.

In comparison with city problems, though, our type of trouble was fairly petty stuff; none the less, the villagers were not prepared to tolerate it. They did not want to suffer fights in the street, vandalism to property in the hall or in the village, discarded beer bottles on the green, cast-off ladies' underwear behind the hedgerows or chip papers dumped in smart gardens. The noises resulting from loud music, revving cars and shouting youngsters were all added nuisances which the people of Aidensfield felt they could do without.

So, after representations from the community, the village hall committee decided it would not allow the premises to be used for weekly dances. Even if the fees did help to pay the bills, it was a chore they could do without.

It was stated though, that the hall could be rented for the annual Hunt Ball and consideration would be given to renting it for specified other dances if the organizers could guarantee good behaviour. In the case of the Hunt Ball, the high price of the tickets kept away the rabble and I never suffered any problems during those events. Similarly, other high-quality organizations rented the hall for their dances, charged high entrance fees or made them all-ticket affairs, and so eliminated bother.

After a period of tranquillity, therefore, the committee saw no reason to deny use of the hall for the annual dance of the Ashfordly, Elsinby and Aidensfield Indoor Plant Society. People who spent their spare time growing plants in greenhouses, conservatories and on kitchen window-sills were hardly the sort to cause public disorder or grievous bodily harm to one another. The committee gave its approval and the dance was arranged for the last Saturday in August. It would run from 8 p.m. to midnight, all dances then having to end before Sunday. There would be a buffet supper and George

Ward gained approval from the magistrates to have a bar in the premises until 10.30 p.m. It was an all-ticket dance and knowing the type of person who would be present I did not foresee any problems. Most of them were genteel people of late middle age whose biggest excitement in life was seeing a *Cymbidium devonianum* burst into flower or nursing an ailing *Kalanchoe beharensis* back to life.

When Inspector Pollock met me on the Wednesday afternoon prior to the dance, he said, 'I see from the duty sheets that you have a dance in the village hall on Saturday? Is this likely to cause a threat to the community? Public disorder? Illicit sales of drugs? Mayhem in the streets? Knifings? Drunkenness?'

'No, sir,' I said with confidence. 'I expect it to be trouble-free,' and I explained the nature of the event, stressing the peaceful qualities of the organizers and the anticipated revellers.

'I can authorize the dog section to be present,' he said. 'Two dogs, two handlers, one van. They're a very good deterrent. And the Task Force ...'

'I can cope on my own, sir,' I assured him. 'I've always managed to deal with problems at local dances, and this is no exception. In fact, so far as policing is concerned, this dance will be the easiest I've had to deal with in years. They're plant enthusiasts, sir. Lovely people. I cannot see them causing trouble anywhere, and certainly not in the streets.'

'Well, all I'm saying is that support is available if you need it, PC Rhea. And I shall be on patrol myself, so I might pay you an official visit.'

'I shall be here, sir,' I said.

On the evening of the great event, therefore, I paid an early visit to the hall and found the massive figure of Jim Blake acting as doorman. Jim was a retired railway worker and was the ideal shape and size to act as bouncer. Single-handed and by his physical appearance alone, he'd keep any crowd of yobbos under control. As we chatted, the dancers were beginning to arrive and I was pleased to see several young people among them. They were probably members of the families of the plant enthusiasts, and they all seemed decent and well-behaved. Inside I could hear the music from a six-piece orchestra as they played old-fashioned dances like the Eva three-step, modern waltz, foxtrot, St Bernard's waltz and other old favourites. This would never attract the ruffians who resorted to such dances simply to cause trouble; I was enjoying the music and my feet were tapping to the gentle rhythms.

By nine o'clock that evening, the hall was full and the music was filling the night air outside. Inside there was the happy sound of chatter as the dancers whirled and frolicked to the music. Even the youngsters were joining in, I noted, and when I popped inside to show my uniform at George's bar, there was a good-natured aura within the hall.

'A nice crowd,' I commented to Jim on the door.

'I wish all dances were as peaceful as this,' he smiled. 'I could have got old Mrs Brownlee to act as bouncer for this and I could have gone to the pub!'

'Are there any more to come?' I asked him.

'A few,' he said. 'Some will have gone to the pub before coming here; they always do that, even though there's a bar here. I close the doors at half-past ten; if you want to get in, knock three times and I'll respond. But I'll allow no more entries after then, even if they have tickets.'

'That'll help to keep trouble at bay!' I said, knowing that a late influx of drinkers was always likely to cause problems even if they were not allowed in.

'Not that we need have worried about this lot!' he beamed.

And so the evening passed in peace and happiness; some youngsters did arrive fairly late, having spent the early part of the evening in the pub, but they were not drunk and Jim permitted them to enter. Then, as he'd told me, he closed the doors at 10.30 and I knew he would not tolerate any further admissions. I decided to potter around the village checking the pub in George's absence, deterring would-be car thieves and generally keeping order.

While I was patrolling in the hot August air, I saw Inspector Pollock's car arrive. He parked immediately before the main door and I went to meet him, slinging up a fine salute.

'All correct, sir,' I chanted as he emerged from his car.

'Good, very good, PC Rhea,' he looked around and saw none of the usual signs of dance-hall bother – no crowds of youths hanging about or lurking in the dark, no giggling girls hiding in corners.

'Would you like to go in, sir?' I asked. 'There is a bar, it's being run quietly and with no trouble.'

'Yes, show me your dance hall, PC Rhea, and all these flower power people.'

As we entered, a pair of youngsters rushed out, brushed past us and shouted 'good night' to Jim Blake. One was a pretty young woman with long blonde hair and dangling ear-rings and the other was a tall young man with dark hair; he wore jeans and a multi-coloured shirt with long sleeves. As the youngsters galloped away, Jim smiled. 'They didn't stay long, they were last in and first out! She must have given him a promise. I wish I was young like that,' he said.

Inside all was peace and calm too; we paraded around the edge of the floor, got kissed by some happy young women, were offered cups of coffee but refused because Pollock would not accept gifts, and checked the bar. It was all quiet and lovely.

'A nice evening, PC Rhea, I'm impressed,' he said. 'I wish I could record the same success at other dance halls. Ashfordly and Strensford could learn from this!'

So the evening continued without incident. At half-past ten, George had to close his bar and at midnight the dance ended, the music stopped and people began to drift homewards. I remained until the band had left, the organizers had counted their takings and Jim had closed the doors.

He had checked the premises – the hall was empty with no one lurking in the toilets, back rooms or bar area. He locked the door and said, 'Well, that's the most peaceful dance I've ever been to, Mr Rhea. What a tonic. Good night.'

And I went home too. It was a quarter-past one as I crept upstairs hoping I would not arouse Mary and the children and by half past one I was fast asleep.

At three o'clock, I was roused by the telephone. It was shrilling in my ear. Thick with sleep I lifted the bedside extension and said, 'Aidensfield Police.'

'Mr Rhea? Look, I'm sorry to bother you, but it's our Glenys, she hasn't come home.'

'Glenys?' I must have sounded dopey but it was difficult to switch my brain into gear having been in such a deep and short sleep.

'It's Ruth Basnett ...'

'Ah, from Elsinby Road.' I knew her husband, Leslie. He was manager of the local Co-op and famed for his collection of rare orchids. He was an authority on the flower and grew them in huge hothouses behind his home.

'Yes, it's our Glenys, she went to the dance and it's unlike her to stay out like this, we're so worried.'

'What time is it?' I muttered.

'Three o'clock,' she said. 'Look, I am sorry, I don't like troubling you, but we're frantic ...'

'I'll come right away,' I promised her.

I muttered something to Mary about being called out but she just grunted in her sleep, and twenty minutes later I was sitting at the Basnetts' kitchen table with a cup of coffee. I was fully awake by now and clad in my uniform.

'So,' I said, 'Glenys said she was going to the dance; she had a ticket and she arrived late.'

'Yes,' said Leslie. 'We said she could come with us, I'm on the committee and had to be there early, but Glenys said she would be meeting some friends who'd be coming to the dance. She said they'd arranged to meet in the pub and come on to the dance later, when everyone had turned up.'

'And did she come later?'

Ruth Basnett, with tears in her eyes, said, 'Yes, I saw her but only briefly. We were at the back of the hall, we were so busy, Leslie and me, with suppers and things; we should have finished serving at half past nine but were kept going until nearly half past ten. We intended leaving the hall by about ten o'clock, once our work was over, we're not dancers, Leslie and I, but we had to keep working for another hour or so, due to the demand. That's when we saw Glenys, just before half-past ten. But we never spoke to her. I saw her across the room, I was at the doorway of the tearoom and I could see across the hall towards the main door, she was near the entrance to the ladies' toilets, standing there. I wondered if she was looking for us, seeing we hadn't gone home by then.'

'Was she alone at that point?' I asked.

'Yes, there was no one with her.'

'And these friends, who were they? Did they come to the dance?'

'She said they were girls she works with, she's at the clothing factory in Strensford. She goes in every day by train. She told us a gang of them said they'd come to the dance with her as a bit of fun; they borrowed one of their dads' cars, she said. Four girls there were. We had tickets waiting at the door, not paid for I might add!'

'And she told you they were all coming to the dance?'

'Yes, that's what she said.'

This puzzled me because I'd not seen a small crowd of young girls at the dance or in the village that evening. During my rounds I had called at George's pub and could not remember seeing the four young women. If they had been there I was sure I would have noticed. The giggles and chatter of a group of excited young women would not have escaped anyone's notice. I must admit I doubted this part of the tale and wondered if Glenys had been meeting a secret admirer.

'Was there a boyfriend among the pals she was meeting?'

'No, she never mentioned one. She hasn't a steady boyfriend, I don't think, not to go out with alone. They go out in groups these days.'

'And what was she wearing? Can you give me a detailed description?'

In my notebook, I began to write down that Glenys was eighteen years old, about five feet five inches tall and of fairly slim build with long fair hair worn loose. She had a fresh complexion and narrow features and was wearing a pair of large, dangling ear-rings in the form of sea shells. She was dressed in a white blouse, a dark blue short skirt and black stockings with black low-heeled shoes. She had a navy blue handbag but, due to the warm evening, had not taken a coat. As the Basnetts gave me these details, I realized they were describing the girl who'd rushed past me and Jim Blake.

She was the girl who had arrived last at the dance and the

one who had left first. Both Jim Blake and I had seen her. But she had been accompanied by a young man, *not* by a group of girls from work. So she *was* keeping secrets from mum and dad!

And if she was with him, I doubted if she would be in any mortal danger. Lustful risks might feature in tonight's adventure, but I did not think she was at risk of death or injury. I wondered if I should mention my own sighting of her and the boy. But for some reason which I shall never know I did not. I did not wish to betray this young woman's personal secrets if she felt it unwise to reveal them.

'I'll circulate this to our patrols,' I assured the distraught parents. 'We won't make too much of a fuss, though, because she is over eighteen and not classed as a juvenile for our purposes. There is nothing to suggest her life is at risk.'

'If she'd gone off with friends, I'm sure she would have told us ... we were at the dance almost till the end, she knew where we were.'

'She might have gone for a ride in her friends' car,' I suggested. 'It might have broken down ... I'm afraid this sort of thing is all part and parcel of having teenagers in the house!'

'It's so unlike her though, Mr Rhea, we don't object to her having boyfriends, or going out, we're broadminded in such things, but she has never been as late as this ...'

In cases of this kind, where adults disappear without reason, we rarely take action simply because they are entitled to go where they want and with whom they want. At that time, the mid nineteen-sixties, a person was not classed as an adult until reaching twenty-one years of age. Glenys was over seventeen and not therefore classified as a child or young person, so she fell between two areas of concern – she wasn't really a missing adult, nor was she a missing child or young person. In spite of the general rules about adults who leave home, so far as young women are concerned there is always an element of risk if they disappear without reason, so I decided I would circulate details of Glenys Basnett.

It was just possible that some of our patrols might have come across an accident or a broken-down vehicle in which she was involved. Before I left the Basnetts' house, though, I asked if her parents knew the names of any of her friends from the clothing factory.

They did not, nor could they describe the car the girls were supposed to have used to drive to Aidensfield. I next rang the hospital and the control room at Strensford police station, but there had been no reports of accidents. Glenys had vanished in mysterious circumstances, so it seemed, and I knew she had been accompanied by a young man, so I assured them I would do all in my power to trace their missing daughter.

I left them huddled over the kitchen table and first did a search of the village, checking parked cars, quiet corners and all the places I knew were used by courting couples, but there was no sign of Glenys. As I made my search I tried to recall more about the youth who'd rushed out of the dance hall with her. It had been in the dark, albeit with the lights of the hall to help a little, and although I felt I'd seen him in the village from time to time, I could not name him.

Back in my office I rang Strensford police station and asked the duty constable to issue a description of the missing girl; I knew this would be circulated among the night patrols of the locality but there was little else I could do. I spent half-an-hour or so completing my notebook and crept upstairs for a few hours' sleep. It was then 4.30 a.m.

The children woke me at 7.30 next morning and as I struggled out of bed my first thought was to ring the Basnetts; but first I rang Strensford police station to see if Glenys had turned up. She hadn't. Next, I rang the Basnetts.

Sounding physically exhausted, Leslie said that Glenys had not come home nor had there been any message. He had searched the village himself and had toured the area in his own car, but had found no trace of her. He said he was at his wits' end and I responded by saying we, the police, would continue our search today.

Then, just before nine o'clock, I received a telephone call from a man called Burton. I knew from the pips and the sound of money dropping into the box that he was ringing from a kiosk.

'Is that t'police?' the strong Yorkshire voice said.

'Yes, Aidenfield Police, PC Rhea speaking,' I responded.

'There somebody fast in one of them garages down near t'old folks bungalows,' he said.

'Trapped you mean,' I asked.

'Aye, locked in. I can hear 'em shouting but can't open t'door, it's locked.'

'Whose is the garage?' I put to him.

'Nobody's, it's a council garage, goes with t'old folks bungalows, but nobody's got it let. It's been empty for months. Number 5 it is.'

'So where will the key be?'

'Council offices at Strensford I should think,' he said. 'Now, I've got to be off, thought I'd better let you know, they're shouting and bellowing from inside, a man and a woman by t'sound of things.'

And the phone went dead, the money having run out. Without wasting any time, I drove down to the little council estate of old folks' bungalows and stopped outside garage No 5. Sure enough, the sound of my approach set off a barrage of shouting from inside, so I tapped on the door and said, 'It's PC Rhea. Who's that?'

A man's voice said, 'Neil Hanby, Mr Rhea, and Glenys Basnett. Can you get us out?'

'Have you a key in there?' I asked.

'No.'

'I'll have to contact the council offices,' I called back. 'It might take a while ...'

'So long as somebody knows we're here,' he said. 'Can you let our parents know? Mine are at Elsinby, Fleetham House.'

'You're not hurt, are you?' I asked. 'Do you need a doctor, ambulance?'

'No, just a toilet!' simpered a girl's voice. 'I'm frozen ...'

'OK, leave it with me,' I assured them. 'We'll soon have you out.'

From my office I rang the council offices at Strensford and after spending twenty minutes finding the right person to answer my question, did learn that a key to No 5 garage was kept there. Next I rang the Basnetts with the good news and then the Hanbys at Elsinby; the Hanbys weren't too worried about their son as he often stayed away from home at night.

I then had to drive into town to collect the key, a return journey of about forty minutes. When I returned to the garage I found the Basnetts waiting outside, holding a conversation with their daughter through the metal door. It was an up-and-over door with a handle in the centre. The centre of the handle accepted the key, rather like the door handle of a motor car, and it was the work of a moment to free the lock and raise the door. Inside, the young couple were momentarily dazzled by the light, because this garage, midway along a block of ten and built of breeze blocks, had no windows.

Then Leslie Basnett realized who the youth was.

'You!' he snarled in a most uncharacteristic way. 'It's you ... you bastard ...'

And he launched himself at the young fellow. Ruth Basnett screamed, Glenys cried that she wanted the toilet and I found myself trying to separate the warring duo. In the ensuing mêlée they fell to the ground with the two women and me doing our best to separate them, but Leslie Basnett's arms and fists were flailing like windmill sails while Neil tried to defend himself against the onslaught.

Between us we managed to separate the pair, with me holding the two contestants at arm's length, shouting at both to cease their warring. At last they did calm down and I relaxed my grip on their collars.

'Les,' I said quietly. 'Glenys is not harmed, she's just a bit tired and needs a wash and a good sleep ...'

'It's not that!' snarled Basnett. 'That bastard ruined my orchids ... last year ... he knows, he daren't show his face near me and yet he dares to court my daughter ...'

'Dad, it was an accident, Neil didn't mean to ...'

'Shut up, all of you!' Ruth entered the fray. 'You're all behaving stupidly. Now just stop it, all of you. Leslie, Glenys needs to get home ... I'm going home with her. PC Rhea, you are welcome to come and have a coffee with us while this escapade is explained, and you, Neil ...'

The young man, his hair awry, his face looking pale and anxious, looked at the formidable lady.

'Yes, Mrs Basnett?'

'I think you'd better join us. Leslie, let old bygones be

bygones, you've got some far better orchids now, prize-winners of a quality that's far better than last year ... so come along, let's all go home and forget about this.'

And so we all went back to the Basnetts' house.

After Glenys had been to the loo we all settled around the kitchen table with Leslie still glaring at Neil; there was deep animosity in that glance.

'So,' I said. 'I need some explanations. Glenys, you first.'

'I wanted to go to the dance with Neil, but I knew dad would never let me go with him, not after that business with the orchids ...'

'You're dead right!' snapped Leslie.

'Be quiet!' his wife demanded. 'Let Glenys say her piece!'

'Well, we went to the pub for a drink, intending to go to the dance when mum and dad had gone home. We thought they were going to leave early, but when we got inside they were still there so we decided to go back outside, to be alone.'

'I didn't want to face Mr Basnett, not after the carry-on with the orchids,' said Neil, blushing. 'So we went outside and just walked around, then we saw the empty garage. It was spotting with rain, so we went inside. The door was open, there was nothing inside and we thought it would be a nice shelter for a few minutes, and then I pulled the door down ... I didn't intend closing it but it suddenly crashed shut. And you can't open those doors from the inside, so we were locked in ... we shouted and shouted, but no one heard us, so we had to stay there all night till that man heard us this morning. He couldn't open it, it had locked itself, like a Yale. It was awful, believe me, dark, nowhere to sit, cold ...'

'All right,' I said. 'Accidents will happen. I can record you as found safe and sound. But Mr Basnett, assaulting a young man like you did means you could be prosecuted for assault or breach of the peace. That's if Neil wishes to press charges.'

'No,' said the youngster. 'I can understand how Mr Basnett felt about those orchids. It was my fault, I deserved it. I just wish I could make amends somehow.'

'Look, I have no idea what happened about the orchids,' I grumbled. 'So can somebody enlighten me?'

I noticed the beginnings of a smile on Basnett's face. 'I

suppose I did over-react,' he admitted. 'But you know I'm a fanatic, a really keen orchid grower?'

'I know you are highly regarded hereabouts as an expert on orchids,' I said.

'Well, the glass got broken in one of the frames of my large hothouse, that one behind the house. I called in a local glazier to refit some glass ...'

'Me,' said Neil. 'My dad's a plumber, we do glazing as well.'

'So this young man came to fix the glass,' sighed Basnett. 'I had to go to work, so I explained exactly what had to be done to maintain both humidity and temperature, but when I got home, he'd left all the doors open. It was a cold, frosty day and I lost hundreds of valuable plants ...'

'No you didn't!' snapped Ruth. 'Most of them recovered, you lost a few, those nearest the door; some failed to flower afterwards, but it wasn't a catastrophe, not by any means.'

'But my orchids did suffer ...'

'He rang my dad up and threatened to do all sort of unmentionable things to me if I showed my face in his hothouses again,' grimaced Neil. 'So you can imagine my reaction when I turned up at the dance with Glenys and saw Mr Basnett was there ... I just turned tail and got out as fast as I could ...'

'And I thought flower growers were a peaceful lot!' I said. 'So, Neil, shall we prosecute Mr Basnett for assaulting you? I need your consent before I can proceed ...'

'No, 'course not,' smiled the youth. 'I was careless. I'm sorry, Mr Basnett. I deserved it, not for keeping Glenys out late but for being careless with your hothouse doors. I never said sorry before, but I do now. I was too scared to ring you or call before ...'

'How about shaking hands?' I said to them both. And after a moment of hesitation, they did. Mrs Basnett hugged her daughter and I could see that there was going to be a few moments of emotion, so I decided to leave. From my office I rang Strensford police station to report the safe return of Glenys Basnett and asked for her name to be crossed off the list of missing persons.

★ ★ ★

Any father will worry when his daughter first attends a dance, whether it is a school dance or one in town where young people congregate. As a policeman and father of three daughters, I could easily understand this concern.

Certainly, a lot of the trouble outside dance halls was due to youths fighting for the favours of a girl but I was still fairly surprised to receive a visit from Robin Mallaby, a newsagent from Ashfordly. He found me in my minivan, patrolling Aidensfield one Friday afternoon, and he hailed me.

'Mr Rhea,' he called after he flagged me down. 'Can you spare a moment?'

'Yes, of course.'

'I'm glad I caught you. You know there's a Young Farmers' dance in your village hall tomorrow?' he said. 'You'll be on duty?'

'Yes, Robin, I'll be there. Why? Are you anticipating a problem?'

'Well, no, not really. But you know my daughter? Charlotte? She works in the shop sometimes, delivers evening papers around Ashfordly.'

'I've seen her, yes,' I agreed. 'A good-looking girl.'

'Yes, well, that's the problem,' he muttered. 'Look, I'm not quite sure how to say this, or I might be over-reacting, but can you keep an eye on her at that dance?'

'An eye on her? Is she in trouble?'

'No, but, well, it's her first dance, Mr Rhea. She's only sixteen, we don't want to stop her enjoying herself, and we can't really go, can we? Not to a dance for youngsters, so if you're on duty, I wondered if you'd just keep an eye on her.'

'Well, I can make sure she comes to no harm, but you can't expect me to forbid her going out with a boy, Robin, that's hardly my job!'

'No, but, well, just pretend you're keeping a fatherly eye on her, make sure she's safe, that none of those ruffians get their hands on her.'

'Well, I'll do what I can if it'll make you happier, Robin.'

'Thanks, that's put my mind at rest ... I do worry about

her, you know ...'

'You're remembering what you did to girls when you were sixteen! That's your problem!' I laughed.

'I know, that's what makes it so bloody hard to let her go, but I know I can't stop her and I wouldn't want to stop her, but it doesn't stop me fretting about her. Damn it, she's just a child.'

'I'll be there, Robin, you sit at home and relax.'

'Aye, well, there won't be much relaxing, not till she's back home and in bed.'

'How's she getting to Aidensfield?' I asked.

'Her cousin's got a car, he's called Maurice, lad of eighteen. He's in the Young Farmers' club and he's taking his own girlfriend, her brother and our Charlotte.'

'I know the lad. OK, Robin, for you I'll keep an eye on her, at a discreet distance, of course!'

And so I found myself agreeing to watch over and protect the sixteen-year-old daughter of a local newsagent. I knew I could never give her my entire protection that evening for I had other duties to perform, but I would keep an eye on the girl, just as I would keep an eye on other vulnerable youngsters that evening. I knew Charlotte by sight and noticed her arrival; she was accompanied by her cousin and his companions. They did not go down to the pub as many others had done, but went straight into the village hall where music was playing. There was a bar in the hall, I knew; it was run by George Ward from the Aidensfield Arms so I knew there would be no bother. At such dances there was often the risk of under-age drinkers being served, thus causing problems later, so I would pop in from time to time to allow the sight of my uniform to act as a warning.

But, like the Ashfordly, Elsinby and Aidensfield Indoor Plant Society's annual dance, this function was completed with the minimum of fuss. I saw Charlotte's burly cousin, Maurice, dancing with his girlfriend, Jill, and her brother Clive had also found a partner whom I did not know. I got the impression he'd come to meet her here because Charlotte did not get many dances. One or two lads twirled her around the floor, but afterwards she sat with Maurice and his party.

Outside the hall, I had to warn one or two merry youngsters about their foul language. I warned some about using the outside of the hall as a public toilet and had to remind others that driving when under the influence of drink could land them in the cells with a court appearance to follow. It was all routine stuff and could not really be classed as a major headache. And then, at quarter to midnight, the dance ended and the cheerful dancers began to leave the premises. I watched them from the comfort of my minivan.

I had parked it in a strategic position, with its lights glowing, so that I could observe a wide area; if there was going to be any real trouble it would occur as the merrymakers were leaving the dance. From the security of my van I could see most of them and, in the event of a real problem, my radio was immediately available.

As the crowds filtered away without any cause for concern, I noticed Charlotte Mallaby. I could see her in the dim glow from a distant street lamp; she was alone and she was standing near Maurice's car, clearly awaiting his return. But the car was locked and she could not get in; I saw her standing somewhat forlornly as the happy crowd evaporated, some arm-in-arm with their new-found friends, others kissing one another and some departing in happy groups.

I decided to wander across and talk to her; in reality, I wanted to make sure she came to no harm. She did look vulnerable and lonely and I found myself recalling her father's concern.

I left my van without bothering to put on my uniform cap – we did not wear caps when in those minivans because the roofs were too low – to wear one's cap in such a tiny vehicle would mean we'd be sitting like hunchbacks! I wandered across to her in the gloom and as I drew near she turned and saw me. I saw a fleeting smile cross her face. She had someone to talk to, even if it was just a policeman. She knew me by sight, for I was a fairly regular visitor to her father's shop, so I asked how she had enjoyed the dance. She began to say she hadn't really enjoyed it.

She'd had no one to dance with and her friends all had other friends to talk to. She'd felt a bit lonely, she said. and then, as

I chatted to her, leaning on the car roof with my elbow, I heard a footfall behind me – someone had crept around the rear of the car and was now approaching. My hair stood on end, a warning of some impending crisis and I whirled around in time to see a massive fist heading for my face. Instinctively I ducked; moving quickly in the manner taught me by our unarmed combat instructor, I seized the outstretched arm, twisted it and succeeded in bringing it high and powerfully up the back of the oncoming assailant. In seconds, I had him on his knees, crying in pain.

'Maurice!' cried Charlotte. 'What on earth do you think you're doing? This is PC Rhea!'

'The policeman?' the big man whispered. 'Oh, God, I'm sorry, Mr Rhea ... I thought it was ...'

I hauled him to his feet and released him; he rubbed his arm as I said, 'You thought it was who?'

'I thought it was somebody annoying Charlotte,' he said meekly.

'Well, even if it was, you don't rush in with all guns blazing before finding out for certain!' I said. 'With a pile-driving fist like yours, you could have felled me – or whoever else it was aimed at.'

Charlotte said, 'Maurice, why? Why won't you let me talk to people? You refused to let me dance with whom I wanted and now this ...'

'Your dad asked me to keep an eye on you,' he told her. 'I was responsible for you! I thought it was somebody pestering you ... I just went over to chat to Alan Cooper about a cattle deal and came back to see you with a man ... I had no idea it was you, Mr Rhea, without your cap ... in the dark ... look, I'm sorry ...'

'Why does dad worry about me so much?' Charlotte cried. 'He's ruined my night out, he's told everybody to keep an eye on me. Everybody! Even the bloody bandsmen were keeping an eye on me! Now, leave me alone, Maurice, take me home. I'm never coming to a dance with you again!'

I daren't tell the poor girl that I had also been keeping an eye on her and that my reason for speaking to her was not one of mere friendship. It was because her father had asked me to watch her.

Maybe all the men at the dance had been watching one another, with requests to report back to her father? No wonder the poor girl had been so alone at her first dance.

'Mr Rhea, I want to apologize,' said Maurice.

'Accepted,' I said. 'Forget it, I'll take no action – this time! But if you go around punching people who chat to your cousin, you're going to finish up in court, or on your back in some gutter with your nose out of joint.'

'Thanks, I'll be careful.'

'And make sure Charlotte enjoys her dance next time, leave her alone,' I said. 'She's grown up now, she can dance with who she wants to, in spite of what her dad says!'

'Thanks, Mr Rhea,' said Charlotte, getting into the car as Maurice unlocked the doors.

'Don't let this put you off going to dances,' I said to her. 'It's just that everyone loves you so much. They don't want to see you come to any harm.'

'I'll try to remember that,' she said, sinking into the rear seat.

And she did go to more dances. Six weeks later I was on duty at the Ashfordly Football Supporters' Club dance and saw Charlotte was there. And she was having a marvellous time. But as I patrolled my lonely beat outside the dance hall I did see her father lurking in the shadows near the Town Hall. Clearly the fellow had some kind of complex about his daughter so I went across to reassure him.

'She'll be safe, Robin, leave her alone, she'll not come to any harm.'

'Somebody attacked my sister at a dance like this, Mr Rhea, years ago when she was sixteen. I can't get it out of my mind. I don't want the same thing to happen to Charlotte.'

'You've not told Charlotte about that, have you?'

'No,' he said.

'Then don't,' I asked him. 'Let her grow up and be happy.'

'It's tough,' he said. 'So bloody tough.'

'I know,' I patted him on the shoulder. 'But youngsters are tough as well. She'll respect you for your love, but don't smother her.'

'Aye, you're right,' and he turned to walk away towards his

shop with the house above the premises. As the dance drew to an end I saw Charlotte walking along the street with a tall and handsome young man.

She did not see me watching from the shadows.

7 *If You Go Down to the Woods Today*

Up he starts, discover'd and surpris'd.
John Milton (1608–1674)

When I was a small child I believed that if I went down to the
woods I would be in for a big surprise. It was all connected
with a popular song about some teddy bears having a picnic in
the woods. Perhaps because of that yearning for a big surprise,
I spent a lot of time in the woods looking for teddy bears
having picnics. I never found any.

There were, however, several fascinating woods around my
childhood village even if I failed to experience that big
surprise. They contained lots of small surprises and pleasures
such as enabling me to discover otter cubs at play, to find
caves, lakes and cliffs, to explore an old ruined millhouse, to
watch salmon and trout swimming against the strong current
of the river, to climb trees and peer into wood pigeons' nests,
to listen to woodpeckers, to scramble up cliffs and poke my
hands into the nests of jackdaws and to touch the eggs as the
female sat on them, to walk nine times around the wishing
stone and then wonder why none of my wishes came true. In
those magical days, I carried a pocket book of British birds
and learned to identify those I saw; in spite of my nesting
exploits I never took or destroyed any birds' eggs.

Another secret I kept was the location of the holt of the
otters whose cubs I watched. I knew that otters were hunted
along that salmon river because they did kill these splendid
fish, but even as a child, I felt I wanted to protect all forms of
wildlife. I was fortunate to grow up in such a wonderful place
and I suppose some would say my childhood was idyllic. For

121

me, though, it was normal. I thought all children had such a
splendid and wide-ranging playground because, in addition to
those woods and rivers, I had the open moors on my doorstep
with expansive views, rugged terrain and untold freedom to
explore. I spent hours in those woods and upon those moors.

It was those superb woods which contained my own secret
place and yet, throughout my childhood, I never did
experience that magical *big* surprise. Maybe all my
experiences were big surprises? How was I to know? As I
matured into my teens and then my twenties, however, I must
admit that those expectations began to evaporate. By the time
I went walking in the woods as an adult, I had forgotten about
big surprises.

But as a young policeman with new stretches of woodland
on my beat at Aidensfield I did in fact experience a curious
surprise – so, after the passage of all those years, that
long-held childhood wish did come true.

It happened one day as I was patrolling through Low
Hollins Wood which bordered the river between Aidensfield
and Thackerston. It was a wonderful place, rich with a variety
of deciduous trees and riddled with interesting footpaths.

I had never walked the length of this wood, either on duty
or off, and on this breezy July day I found myself with a
couple of hours to spare. I was on duty and decided to
acquaint myself with the geography of the woodland and its
maze of paths just in case I ever had to search it for any reason.
I considered that a detailed knowledge of its terrain should be
gained as part of my local knowledge; it was in my professional
interest to know every inch of my beat, I told myself.

Off I went, therefore, in full uniform, to explore the main
footpath. The wood was noisy with birdsong and the
movement of animals in the undergrowth; I could hear the
sound of tiny creatures like shrews and wood mice, I caught
sight of a fox lurking behind some rhododendrons and knew
that badgers had a safe haven nearby. I watched a green
woodpecker hammering on a dead tree in search of grubs and
spotted two jays, the most shy of birds, flitting among a small
group of conifers. Wood warblers and willow warblers,
blackbirds, spotted flycatchers, tree-creepers, wood pigeons,

pheasants, a kestrel – those and more were in that wood, some sounding their alarm calls at my intrusion into their territory and others almost ignoring my presence. It was rather like a re-run of some of my childhood joys.

But then I saw a very strange but handsome bird. I caught a mere glimpse of it but in that fleeting moment gained the impression that it was about the size of a pheasant with a long, feathery tail and dark bottle-green plumage. It flew across the path ahead of me and its flight appeared to be clumsy, rather like that of a pheasant. Pheasants are not the most agile of birds when in the air and this bird appeared to be similarly cumbersome. None the less, it did clear the shrubs ahead of me before it vanished into the undergrowth.

I was baffled. It was not like any British bird that I knew. I realized that exotic birds did escape from captivity from time to time, and some people in the district did breed ornamental pheasants. I wondered if this was one that had escaped. I could have been wrong, of course, for I had gained but a very fleeting glimpse of the bird, so I was unsure what it was. But the sighting did arouse my interest and I concentrated upon trying to see it again.

I decided I would follow the direction the curious bird had taken, so I diverted from the main footpath and followed a far less well defined one. I must have walked for about a quarter of a mile when another strange-looking bird bolted from the undergrowth, half flew and half scrambled through a patch of briars and then disappeared with a cackling noise. It was more of a russet colour and did not look like the first one, although there were similarities, the chief one being the clumsy attempt at flight. Now I was very interested in these odd birds. I racked my brains in an effort to identify them, but failed to produce a name. I wished I'd had my bird book!

Without going into too much detail about the experiences which followed, it is fair to say that during the next hour I came across about a dozen strange birds, none of which was like any other except that all had the same clumsy method of flying. Their colours were varied – I saw one which was pure white and very heavy, another with greys and yellows dominating, a grey one and a tiny, cheeky looking thing with green plumage below and reddish-brown above. From time to time I noticed one which seemed similar to earlier sightings and could not decide whether I had seen the same bird twice, or whether this was another. As I had sighted the creatures some distance from my first experience, I guessed that, for each colourful bird, there were several examples in this wood.

As I found more of these odd birds during that ramble through the deep, quiet part of this wood, I thought they looked like cockerels or even fighting cocks. To my knowledge, however, the awful and highly illegal sport of cockfighting was not practised in this area, although rumours of its existence in some parts of rural Yorkshire did persist. But no breeder of fighting cocks would risk rearing his valuable birds in the wild like this.

If these were all cock birds, though, where were the hens? How were they breeding? I felt sure there were no hens around and was equally unsure whether these were some exotic breed or several exotic breeds which had reverted to the wild.

Another factor to consider was whether new species of wild birds had come to this country since my knowledgeable childhood days. I knew that this did happen – birds moved around the world in quite an astonishing way and exotic or rare species did sometimes find their way to Britain.

Whatever they were, these birds were very shy and they were not domesticated; they concealed themselves from view and flew away at the slightest hint of danger, just like any other wild bird, so I never achieved a really good view of any one of them. All my sightings were brief, too brief to really secure a proper description, but as I explored that part of Low Hollins Wood I began to realize there was a colony of these strange birds, with many different types living here. I had not counted the numbers of different varieties I'd seen, but guessed it was about a dozen, in some cases with two or more examples of the same bird.

Baffled, I decided it was time to return to the village. I had not reached the far end of the footpath but my short period of exploration had come to an end because time had run out. As I walked back my mind was ranging aross the varieties of large game birds such as pheasant, capercaillie, partridge or even the tiny quail, but none fitted the description of my sightings. I was convinced they looked very much like farmyard cockerels but their colours were far more exquisite and, of course, they were wild birds.

As I entered Aidensfield luck was on my side because, emerging from the post office, was the familiar figure of Albert Firth, chairman of the Ryedale Hen Watching Society. In his late seventies, Albert was a mine of information about domestic poultry and had been chairman of the society for more than fifty years. The ancient and highly active group of experts held regular meetings about all aspects of domestic poultry, listening to lectures about their history, breeding, care, behaviour and lore. Society members kept observations upon hens in the domestic situation, keeping detailed records of their behavioural traits, language, nesting habits and the effect of the moon and the wind upon egg-laying. In addition, the society discussed difficult problems such as whether eggs with brown shells are more nutritious than those with white ones, why hens always take two steps backwards after scratching for grubs, whether mood music affects egg-laying, whether the feathers of a cockerel's tail make good flies for fishermen and a whole range of similar topics. One of the problems which caused immense discussion was why hens run across the road when a car is approaching. No one has yet found a satisfactory answer and it is the theory of the society that not even hens know why they cross the road.

'Now then, Mr Rhea,' said the ruddy-faced Albert when he saw me approaching.

'Now then, Albert,' I returned the traditional greeting. 'Not a bad day for the time of year.'

'It could be better and it could be worse,' he nodded gravely.

'It could indeed,' I agreed with him. 'But we've got to take what we've got, we can't change it. There's always something different happening with our weather.'

'Aye,' he nodded. 'And there's allus a lot of weather about at this time of year.'

'True,' I muttered. 'Well, Albert, I'm really pleased I

caught you. I need the benefit of your expertise on hens. I've come across some very strange birds down Low Hollins Wood,' and I explained what I had just seen, adding that they did look very like unusual types of cockerels.

'They're not hoopoes or rollers, are they?' he suggested.

'No,' I said firmly. 'I know what they look like.'

'Ornamental pheasants? Lady Amherst's pheasants? Silver pheasants?'

'Nope,' I shook my head. 'They don't have the long tails of pheasants.'

'Well, that caps hen racing,' he said.

'Could they be fighting cocks gone wild?' I suggested.

'Not in all them colours you mentioned,' he shook his old head. 'And you say there were no hens?'

'They didn't look like hens to me,' I said, adding, 'But I'm no expert, Albert. They might have been hen birds of some species I've never come across.'

'Well, if there's no hens, they'll not be breeding, will they?'

'That's true,' I admitted.

'Nor laying eggs,' he added.

'True,' I agreed.

'Nor nesting.'

'No,' I had to admit.

'That's a rum 'un, if they're not nesting either,' he was thinking seriously now. 'Now, that is a fair capper, Mr Rhea. I'd better get myself down there for a look.'

I gave him directions to the spot where I'd seen most of the birds and he said he would take a walk down there this afternoon. I left him to go about his business as I continued my patrol, now engaging myself on more conventional police work. I had an appointment to interview a witness to a road accident which had occurred in Middlesbrough a week earlier and therefore made my way to the witness's house.

It would be a week later when I next saw Albert and he hailed me with a huge wave of his hand. I halted my van and climbed out.

'Now then, Mr Rhea,' he said.

'Now then, Albert,' I returned.

'Not a bad day for the time of year,' he smiled. 'And I

shouldn't be surprised if it rains before night.'

'It'll do a bit of good,' I said. 'We need a bit of rain, things are very dry.'

'Aye, you're right. Well, what I stopped you for was this. I went down Low Hollins Wood and saw them birds.'

'Oh, good. So what's your opinion?' I put to him.

'Cock birds,' he said. 'They're all cock birds, different breeds, all living wild down there.'

'You mean ordinary domestic cockerels?' I was surprised.

'Not ordinary ones, Mr Rhea. Decorative ones. Did you know there's more than seventy species of domestic hen? And as many species of cock birds? All descended from *gallus gallus*, that's the red jungle fowl that still lives wild in some parts of Asia.'

'No, I never knew that,' I had to admit.

'Well, that's summat you've learned. Now them birds down Low Hollins Wood, they're all species of cock birds, different ones, all living wild.'

'Don't they fight for territory?' I sought expert advice on this.

'I wouldn't be surprised if there was a bit of jockeying for position,' he said. 'Boss bird an' all that. Anyroad, that's what they are. Cock birds living wild. Probably with their own bit of woodland as territory, but all staying in one spot or near enough to one spot.'

'But Albert, this raises more questions. How did they get there? If they're all cockerels, how are they sustaining their numbers?'

'You've got me now, Mr Rhea,' and he shook his head.

'So you don't think it's got anything to do with any of your members?' I suggested.

'Nay, lad, I would think not. Our folks would never turn good cocks into t'wild like yon.'

'So where could they have come from?'

'Now that's a right capper. I couldn't rightly say, but I'll tell you what. Next time our society has a meeting, I'll see if anybody knows owt about them birds. But you'd think we would know, being the only Hen Watching Society hereabouts.'

'Exactly my sentiments, Albert.'

'Aye, well, it's summat for t'society to get their teeth into, it'll stop 'em arguing about whether free range eggs is better than them from battery hens, or whether hens can see t'colours of traffic lights. Now that happened because awd Mrs Rymer from Rigg Top Farm reckoned her hens would never cross t'road when t'red light was showing on some road works up yonder. Makes you think, that sort o' thing, Mr Rhea.'

'It does indeed, Albert. There's something I've always wondered as well. That's whether hens can recognize their own names. When I was a child, we had pet hens, you see, one called Clara Cluck, another was Bunty Chops and another was Biffy. When we took their food out and called their names, they all came running. I often wonder what would have happened if we'd only shouted for Clara Cluck.'

'By gum, Mr Rhea, that's a puzzler, it's summat else we can discuss. Can hens recognize their own names? That'll keep our members going for weeks and I reckon some'll want to run tests with their own stock. Thanks, it's a good subject.'

'Well, thanks for your help, Albert,' I said. 'It would be nice if we knew why those birds were living there, so I'll make my own enquiries too. I'll let you know if I discover anything.'

'Aye, right you are, Mr Rhea. Now while I've got you here there's a matter to settle about them cocks in yon wood. You're not interested in them from an official police point of view, are you? I mean, have they been stolen from somewhere? Are they t'proceeds of crime, is that why you're interested? Keeping 'em under observations in case t'thief comes back for 'em, perhaps?'

'To my knowledge, Albert, they are not the subject of any crime. We've had no reports of any stolen cockerels, I think we would have known if exotic or rare ones had been stolen. I just happened to come across them the other week and was curious about them, that's all. It's a personal puzzle.'

'Well, it's just that there's a lot of good blood stock going to waste down there and some of our members' hens might enjoy meeting them lads. I did wonder what the position would be if we rounded 'em up and brought 'em into domestic use.'

'I can't see anything wrong with that,' I said. 'They're not a protected species of wild bird, and they don't have an owner, so it appears. So I can't see why you shouldn't try to capture them, although they're a bit cunning, I reckon.'

'Not as cunning as some of our chaps, though,' he grinned. 'In fact, one of our members is just the fellow to round them up for us. He's an expert in that sort of thing.'

'Who's that?' I asked.

'Claude Jeremiah Greengrass,' he said. 'He keeps hens, you know, and is very knowledgeable. It was him who reckoned his hens prefer brown bread to white bread, and he reckons if you feed 'em with brown bread, it makes 'em lay brown eggs while white bread produces white eggs.'

'I've never heard that before,' I told him, adding, 'But a lot of hens never eat bread at all, do they?'

'Nay, you've got a point there, Mr Rhea,' smiled Albert. 'Well, I'd better be getting along. You've given me a lot to think about, a lot for the Ryedale Hen Watching Society to discuss and test. They might even make you a member, Mr Rhea. How about that?'

'I should be very honoured, Albert,' I said. 'But I don't keep any hens now.'

'You don't have to keep hens to qualify, Mr Rhea, you've just got to be interested. We're a Hen Watching society, not Hen Keeping society. You've just got to study and watch 'em and I reckon you'll see a lot of hens when you're on duty.'

'Well, we do see a lot which are injured, Albert. In road accidents, generally. Did you know that a hen is not classed as an animal for road accident purposes?'

'Nay, I never knew that!'

'Well, it means we have no statistics about hen casualties on the roads, so the society might be able to campaign for hens to be classified as animals, like dogs, goats, cattle, horses, asses, mules, pigs and sheep.'

'Not cats?' he asked.

'Not cats or hens,' I said. 'Nor even ducks, geese, turkeys or peacocks for that matter.'

'By gum, you learn summat every day! You would be a very useful chap to have on our committee, Mr Rhea. Knowing the law like you do. Now, talking about the law, if you see Claude Jeremiah Greengrass chasing hens in yon wood, you won't arrest him for poaching, will you?'

'Not if he gets permission to take them. He'll have to inform the owner of the wood. It's part of Elsinby estate, isn't it?'

'Aye, right, good thinking, Mr Rhea.'

'If he gets permission from the landowner, it means he's not trespassing, Albert, and if he's not trespassing, it means he can't be prosecuted for trespassing in pursuit of game, just in case some bright spark thinks those cockerels are game birds. Maybe a note from the chairman of your society authorizing him to round them up might be a good idea?'

'By gum, that's me, that's another bright idea!' beamed Albert and so he trotted off to organize the great cockerel round-up.

I thought I had better have words about this charade with the gamekeeper for Elsinby estate and found him in the estate office the following morning. A genial man, he was called Doug Thorpe and invited me to join him for a coffee. As I enjoyed his hospitality, I explained about the curious birds in Low Hollins Wood and he smiled.

'Oh, those, Nick. Sure, I know about them. Actually, they've become a bit of a nuisance now. There's rather too many. Some of them get a bit frisky and they're moving towards the farms and villages, to have a go at the hens. Some farmers have been getting very strange chicks!'

'Where have they come from?' I asked.

'It's a chap from Strensford, I think, he's a breeder of chickens and has dozens of varieties, so he says. Well, when his broods hatch, he always has too many cockerels. As you know, most farmers destroy any surplus cock chickens but well, this chap can't bring himself to do that. So instead of wringing their necks, he releases them in the wild. He never asked us permission to dump them in our wood, but I caught him one day and well, I couldn't see why he shouldn't release one or two. But I never got his name or address, so I don't know who he is or how to get in touch with him. Anyway, he keeps coming back when I'm not around and dumps a few more.'

'So there's generations of cock-birds living in that wood?'

'There is, it's been going on for a few years now, Nick.'

'Well, Doug, I've got news for you,' I told him. 'The Ryedale Hen Watching Society wants to round up a few of those birds for their own domestic purposes.'

'They're welcome to as many as they can catch!' he expressed a sigh of relief.

'There's only one problem,' I added, tongue in cheek.

'What's that?' he frowned.

'Their chief rounder-up of hens will be none other than Claude Jeremiah Greengrass,' I said.

'Well, so far as rounding up game birds goes, they couldn't have found a chap with more skill, but I'm not sure I can trust him to be at large in our woods! He might get his eye on some of our pheasants instead!'

'I suppose if he was supervised, it would help?' I put to him.

'I could help him,' said Doug. 'Yes, that's it. Tell whoever's making the arrangements to get in touch with me and I'll help Claude to round up a few of those cockerels. I'll be glad to see the back of them, to be honest.'

'If we can find out who the phantom cockerel depositor is,' I suggested, 'we could ask him to get in touch with the Ryedale Hen Watching Society direct, I'm sure they'd take some good specimens off his hands instead of him having to leave them to fend for themselves.'

'If I see him, I'll tell him,' said Doug.

And so Claude Jeremiah Greengrass found himself performing an authorized type of poaching, using his skills with nets and brandy-filled raisins to round up a few wild cockerels. The trick was to persuade the cockerels to eat lots of the brandy-filled raisins, which would make them drunk and fall asleep. It was easy thereafter to collect them, pop them into hessian sacks and deliver them to Albert Firth and his society members.

So far as I know, the phantom dumper of the cockerels was never located, but new birds did continue to arrive in that wood, whereupon the society would capture them with the aid of Claude Jeremiah and the Estate.

For my efforts I was made an honorary member of the

Ryedale Hen Watching Society. I was quite pleased by this because membership of such an august society might enable me to discover whether it is possible to house-train a pet hen.

★   ★   ★

I was to call upon Claude Jeremiah's woodcraftsmanship on another occasion. It was a quiet summer morning when someone knocked on my police office door. When I opened it, I found Claude Jeremiah outside looking as pale as a piece of putty and visibly shivering.

'By gum, Mr Rhea, I've had summat of a shock ...'

'You look shattered, Claude, what is it?'

'I'll have to come and sit down,' he said. 'My legs are like jelly ... I nearly died out there, so I did.'

'Has somebody taken a pot shot at you?' I wondered if he'd been on a poaching expedition or engaged upon some other nefarious deed.

'Nay, worse than that. I nearly got blown to bits. Up in Howe Plantation.'

He was literally quivering with fright so I invited him into the office and called through to Mary to make him a hot, strong coffee with lots of sugar. I said I'd have one too, though not quite so sweet.

When he'd calmed down and was drinking the coffee I asked for an account of his experience. It seemed that, for some reason he declined to explain, he had been walking with his lurcher, Alfred, in Howe Plantation early that morning. It had been about half past seven, when he was homeward bound, that his boot had caught a metal object which was almost entirely buried. Thinking he might have stumbled across some concealed treasure, he'd begun to scrape away the earth with a piece of wood when he realized what the object was. It was an unexploded bomb from the Second World War; it was German, four feet long and apparently in a very fragile condition.

At that point, he'd run for his life.

The bomb had not exploded and after he'd had a stiff whisky at home he decided to report his discovery. Clearly the fellow had been shocked, but for the police of the North York moors this was a fairly regular occurrence in the years following the Second World War.

The moors were littered with discarded bombs and shells because when the Germans had flown over them towards Teesside during their raids, they sometimes completed their missions over the target area without dropping all their payload. The surplus bombs were jettisoned on the homeward run. Many of them fell on to the open moors and failed to explode; some lay buried for years, often in a state where they were capable of exploding and causing considerable damage.

Another reason for the large crop of bombs on the moors, in both an exploded and unexploded condition, was that during the Second World War false towns were established on the remoter heights. These consisted of nothing more than large groups of makeshift buildings with lights, set in the middle of the moors. At night-time, from a high-flying plane, they had all the appearances of townships. The incoming Germans dropped their precious bombs on these places – a useless exercise. Even today unexploded bombs (UXBs) are still discovered on the moors, especially in the soft, marshy areas. Claude had found one of them.

For the police the procedure was simple. We had to identify the precise location of the discovery, mark it in some way so that the bomb disposal experts could locate it, and keep the public away.

Howe Plantation, on the moors to the west of Aidensfield, was shown on recent Ordnance Survey maps of the district, and after discussion with Claude about the most suitable route to the bomb I was able to pinpoint the general area. I would, however, require Claude's presence to guide the military experts to its precise position. I rang Sergeant Blaketon to inform him of the discovery and said I would deal with it; my next task was to call the Bomb Disposal Unit of the Royal Engineers at Catterick Camp. They dealt with reports of all foreign or enemy bombs while the Ministry of Defence, Directorate of Weapon Engineering, dealt with reports of British or Allied bombs.

I rang them and made my report; they wanted to speak to

Claude to establish as much detail as possible, and finally we agreed to a rendezvous on the southern edge of Howe Plantation. The maps showed a rough track to that point and the Bomb Disposal Unit spokesman said his men would arrive at that location by 11 a.m. I assured him that Claude and I would be there to meet his team.

'You're not expecting me to go back there, Mr Rhea, are you?' He was still nervous.

'No one else can tell us where to find this infernal machine,' I said. 'And I thought you'd done service in the army, I thought you'd undertaken all manner of dangerous missions and daring deeds on behalf of the country.'

'Aye, well, mebbe I did, when I was younger and dafter, but this is dangerous work, Mr Rhea.'

'No it isn't! All we require of you is to show us precisely where the bomb is, you don't have to touch it or go near it. If you don't show us, it could kill somebody.'

And so he agreed.

In my police minivan, Claude and I, accompanied by the faithful Alfred, arrived some twenty minutes before the appointed rendezvous time. I was surprised to see an open-topped military jeep standing at the meeting point. It was occupied by a driver and a major both clad in camouflaged outfits. The major leapt out and came towards me.

'Ah, Constable, you are on routine patrol here?'

'No, not really, not routine ...'

'Then I wonder if I might ask you to depart, we are engaged upon a secret escape and evasion exercise in this plantation, we start at eleven, we must secure the entire area. It's the SAS, top secret work, you understand, we are guarding all entrances to the forest to prevent unauthorized access.'

'But ...' I began.

'I have seniority here, Constable, I am a major in Her Majesty's Special Air Services and I am in command. This is a military operation. I must ask you both to leave.'

'You have men in this wood?' I asked.

'Yes, a dozen, they are already concealed and camouflaged, they must not be taken by a team of 'enemy' invaders who are due at eleven o'clock ... the invaders will comb this wood for my men, and my men must evade them at all costs.'

'And I am here because this friend of mine, Mr Greengrass, has discovered an unexploded German bomb in this plantation.'

'You tell him, Mr Rhea!' chipped in Claude.

'Oh my God!' The major went a ghastly shade of white.

'I have called the Bomb Disposal Unit at Catterick,' I went on. 'They are due to arrive at eleven o'clock to deal with the bomb. We are here to show them where it is.'

'But I have spent months organizing this exercise, it's vital for my unit ...'

'It seems to me that you will have to cancel or postpone it,' I said. 'I should hate any of your men to tread on Claude's bomb. It might just explode and it would blow a huge hole in these moors if it did. And the Germans might claim it had killed a few British soldiers!'

'I can't call it off,' the major spoke weakly. 'My men are all concealed in this plantation, there's about ten square miles and I have no idea where they are. I cannot contact them because they have no radios. They are all hidden and will remain concealed until eleven o'clock tomorrow morning – unless they are located and captured by the enemy.'

'But surely they'll emerge if we can get a message to them?' I suggested. 'Loudhailers or something.'

'No, whatever you do, they'll think it is a piece of trickery by the enemy, that's what they have been told. They know the enemy will make use of all kinds of devices and devious tactics to persuade them to leave their hiding-places and get caught. They will resist every move which encourages them to show themselves.'

'So when will they come out?' I asked.

'Tomorrow. Those who are not caught will rendezvous here, with me, at eleven tomorrow morning.'

'If the bomb is made secure, there will be no problem,' I said. 'But if it goes off, it could kill everyone within range – and I've no idea what the range of this bomb is. If any of your men are hiding within range of it, they could be killed. Surely you have some official and acceptable means of recalling your men?'

'Well, actually no,' he admitted. 'We haven't. The only way they can be persuaded to emerge is if they are arrested by the enemy, who will be arriving soon for their briefing.'

'So that means we shall have to find and arrest them all before the bomb can be made safe? But if one of them treads on the bomb or disturbs it during their exercise, it could go off and kill several. It has been partly uncovered already.'

Claude had been listening to us during these useless exchanges and said, 'PC Rhea, if I went into that wood with Alfred, we could find 'em. We're good at tracking, we're a crack team, me and Alfred.'

'You?' I smiled.

'I mean it. I'm the best. Me and Alfred that is. We could search the area within range of that bomb and arrest 'em all.'

'Could you really?' I must have sounded surprised.

'Aye, course I can. Us old soldiers have to stick together, eh, Major? Alfred would point 'em out to me, he'd tell me where they were hiding, he's good at that sort o' thing, flushing out them that thinks they're well hidden.'

'You'd need one of the enemy soldiers with you,' said the major. 'They have a coloured tag on their uniforms, the concealed men know what colour it is.'

'Colour sergeants, are they?' blinked Claude, jokingly.

The major ignored this and said, 'Those colours will authenticate an enemy soldier. They will only submit to soldiers wearing those tags, everyone else will be regarded as a decoy and thus ignored or even captured and held until the conclusion of the exercise. They would be regarded as collaborators.'

Minutes later some army vehicles carrying two dozen soldiers with rifles and in heavy camouflage came to a halt at our point. The 'enemy' had arrived. They were followed by a smaller vehicle bearing a sign saying 'Bomb Disposal Unit' and sporting a blue light. A captain and a sergeant disembarked from the latter while another major descended from the 'enemy' vehicle. The officer in charge of each arrival wondered what the other was doing in this vicinity and there followed some rather intense and heated discussions between the assembled parties.

The captain in command of the Bomb Disposal Unit stressed that under no circumstances could the escape and evasion exercise continue with an unexploded bomb in the middle of it. Some wit said it would add an air of reality to the exercise, especially as it was a genuine enemy bomb, but after a lot of hot air, swearing, discussions about army protocol and procedures, it was decided that Claude must first show the captain the bomb. The captain would then make an assessment upon which to order any further action.

So we all trooped into the plantation of young conifers, plodding along an identifiable but little-used footpath for about four hundred yards until Claude halted. Alfred halted at his side and sniffed the air. Claude then pointed ahead and there, some ten yards away and very close to the edge of the footpath, was the distinct shell of a bomb. It was clearly showing where Claude had scraped away the peaty earth and seemed to be in reasonably good condition with little rust or serious deterioration.

The bomb disposal wizards crept forward to carry out their preliminary inspection. It took them but a few seconds to declare that the bomb was a relic of the Second World War; it was German, it was not particularly large or powerful, but it was alive. Closer inspection showed that the fuse was still in position and there was some slight corrosion; it could, in fact explode at any time. It wouldn't require much to set it off.

'I'm off!' said Claude.

'Me too,' I said.

And at that point Alfred wandered towards the bomb. Claude saw him and yelled, 'Alfred, you daft bat! Come here. Here, heel ...'

But Alfred ignored his lord and master, if only for a few seconds. He instinctively approached the bomb, sniffed at it while those present held their breath, then he cocked his leg and directed a steady stream at the bomb. Thus he had marked the bomb; it was now upon Alfred's territory.

'Alfred!' There was pain and worry in Claude's voice, and Alfred then came to heel. At this stage the captain, whose name was Chambers, advised everyone to get well away from the bomb; the vehicles we had left on the track should be at a safe enough distance, he said. They were parked in a hollow, the edge of which provided a barrier between them and the bomb. He reckoned that if the bomb did explode it could kill at three hundred yards, with flying rocks and debris being a danger over a far greater distance, even up to five or six hundred yards, although that danger would be lessened by the density of the growing conifers.

The trees near the bomb would be destroyed, but those at a distance would act as a barrier to the effect of the blast, as would mounds of earth which were dotted around the forest. Many trees could withstand such a blast, depending upon their distance from the point of the explosion. He said he felt confident that the bomb would not explode unless it received a severe knock or direct hit; he also said he felt sure he could defuse it and make it safe without an explosion. Nevertheless, the problem of the concealed soldiers remained. If the bomb did explode, any soldiers hidden within a hundred yards of it could be killed. And they would resist any moves to tempt them out of hiding simply because they thought that such pleas were trickery.

'Can you really find them, Claude?' I asked him.

'Aye,' he said. 'Me and Alfred can. We can find 'em, using our sixth sense. I was a wartime scout, me, tracking through the jungles of Burma and moving like a wraith ... But I can't track with a bomb waiting to go off!'

'It won't go off unless it's knocked or damaged,' said Captain Chambers. 'I can assure you of that. It will be perfectly safe unless it receives a severe knock. I'll stand near the bomb while you do a recce within four hundred yards. Any soldier you find will be considered taken by the enemy – but as I said earlier, you must be accompanied by an enemy soldier suitably marked.'

And so Claude found himself exercising his considerable tracking skills in the wood, aided by the sensitive nostrils of Alfred his lurcher and accompanied by an 'enemy' soldier.

Together they found five soldiers hiding within range of the bomb and these were 'captured' by the enemy; Alfred angered one of them by peeing upon his helmet as he lay prone. It seemed Alfred liked marking things in his own specialized manner. Then a loud-hailer message was broadcast to those who were not caught, warning them of an unexploded bomb. The location was given. Captain Chambers moved in quickly, saying it would take at least an hour to complete his work, and so the testing time began. We all worried that the soldiers who had not been found might begin to move around, but that was a risk which had to be taken. But Chambers did a good job. By one o'clock, he had defused the bomb, saying it had been in remarkably good condition and that the fuse had been somewhat complicated. It could have exploded but it was now safe. The exercise could continue.

The SAS major was not very pleased that his men had been found by a poacher and his dog; the enemy major said that if a local man and his dog could find the concealed soldiers, then so could his experts, while Captain Chambers thanked Claude for his assistance. He showed his appreciation to Alfred too, by giving him a bar of chocolate; Alfred showed his appreciation by raising his leg against the wheel of his vehicle.

And so our drama was over. Claude was silent on the way back to Aidensfield, clearly thinking over what might have happened. I told him how pleased I was that he had volunteered his services in that way – he could have saved a life.

'There's only one thing bothering me,' he said at length. 'Me being an old soldier, like.'

'What's that, Claude?' I asked.

'I was working for the enemy wasn't I? Helping them to find our men. Me, a good, loyal member of His late Majesty's forces.'

'But you helped to defuse a real enemy bomb,' I reminded him.

'Aye, so I did. Me and Alfred. Alfred doesn't remember the war, Mr Rhea, he wasn't even born then.'

'He'd have made a good spy,' I said. 'The Allies could have dropped him in France. I wonder if he likes parachutes?'

8   Ladies of the Village

When he has ladies to please, every feature works!
Jane Austen (1775–1817)

Police officers and authors have one thing in common – they
enjoy observing people.

For the police officer on foot patrol, the practice of watching
people going about their daily routine can be both productive
and fascinating. The productive side comes from knowing
what is happening on one's patch and many a crime has been
solved through the observational skills of a uniformed
constable. Knowing who the person was and why he or she
was at that place at that time has always been a good aid to the
detection of crime.

The fascination comes from studying, in very real terms,
the behaviour of human beings. One peculiarity is that one
sees the same people in the same place each day; they are
buying the same items from the same grocer's, they are seen
sitting on the same park bench to rest their feet or catching the
same bus back home after standing at the same bus stop facing
the same way while carrying the same shopping bag.

We are all creatures of habit and we do not realize that
others are keenly aware of those habits; it is only when we
cease to follow our daily pattern that others miss us.

Many old folk have been saved from death because
neighbours and friends have noted that these vulnerable
members of society have not undertaken their daily rituals. If
old Mr Brown isn't buying his bread at the usual time, his
absence is noted and becomes a cause for alarm; if Mrs Green
doesn't come into the post office at 10.15 a.m. on Thursday

140

like she always does, we worry about her; if Mr Grey is walking along the street without the overcoat he wears every day of the year, then we know he's having problems and we do something about it.

One skill which develops from years of observing others is that it is sometimes possible to foretell a person's next move. Many is the time I have been standing on a street corner, knowing that a motorist is going to turn left or right in spite of that driver never having signalled his or her intention. There is some indefinable indication in the way the car and its driver behave that provides a clue to the immediate future.

Likewise, one instinctively knows that the lady walking in front of you will suddenly stop, turn around and hurry back to the shop she has just left; one knows that a child on the pavement will suddenly dart across the road or that the old lady with the puzzled frown on her face and clutching a pile of cheap novels will ask for directions to the nearest library. Groups of little old ladies always manage to get lost in shopping precincts and bus stations, old men catch the wrong trains and young mums often manage to lose infants in crowded places. Tourists always ask for directions to the car parks, the toilets and the nearest café, while Americans ask the way to Buckingham Palace, Scotland or Herriot country.

One interesting pastime when observing the public is to try to work out a person's occupation from their appearance; this is particularly fascinating if travelling by InterCity train, when one may spend up to two hours sitting opposite another traveller. Business men with notions of their own importance in the world are readily identifiable by their smart suits, black briefcases and statutory portable telephones, even if they are merely going to a seminar about brass screws or a new range of scented air-fresheners. Others are not so easy to identify.

Teachers are fairly easy to pick out, as are off-duty police officers, nurses or fire officers. Salesmen and saleswomen often look harassed but especially so if the train is even two minutes late; they usually have piles of forms which need to be filled in at every minute of the day. Holidaymakers tend to be excited and noisy, people going for interviews or exams are nervous and read their notes over and over again, pensioners read the *Sun* because they can't afford anything else, shoppers repeatedly make new lists of their requirements and students spend their time walking the corridors drinking from cans of lager or coke they've brought on board. Male students will walk time and time again past a group of pretty female students, hoping to make some favourable impression. European nationals seem to think that every seat is booked automatically upon purchase of one's ticket and Scotsmen speak in long sentences of incomprehensible dialect which is delivered with the speed of a machine gun. Long train journeys are a rich source of material for authors.

Shoes are often a give-away to a person's status in the world, highly polished ones indicating someone in a position of importance, casual ones revealing someone who pays more attention to comfort than appearance and those with thick soles indicating a person with a complex about their lack of height. I think the modern term for short people is 'vertically challenged' – I'm not sure what the term is for people who dream up such political daftness.

Authors tend to observe others in a continual search for characters suitable for inclusion in their novels. There are times when a person's appearance can be deceptive – it is easy for a writer to look at a smart person and then to describe the style of clothing. It takes a vastly different technique to understand the character who is wearing those clothes – to create a totally fictitious character so that the person appears to be real, with feelings and ambitions, is never easy. In fact, it is extremely difficult.

Many authors tend to base their creations on people they know well or whom they meet during their travels. Quite often, for example, a very smart and confident appearance will conceal a confidence trickster; an old person in cheap, ragged clothing might be a titled and wealthy individual; the fun-loving, chip-eating buffoon you meet on holiday might well be a highly successful company director back home while the man with dark glasses and a pipe might be a detective watching us all.

It was this habit of observing others that drew my attention to the curious world of Miss Mabel Hibbard, sometimes known to the children of Aidensfield as Old Mother Hubbard. She was a rather squat and heavily built lady with iron-grey hair done in a bun and she always wore a heavy royal blue overcoat; she topped it with a curious old-fashioned hat. Her bun protruded from the back of her hat rather like a rabbit's tail.

She always carried a round shopping basket with nothing inside. Her shoes were flat and well-worn, while her stockings were of old-fashioned lisle and full of wrinkles. She walked with a slight limp in her left leg; her gait was rather like that of a rolling sailor. Even so she would walk very rapidly, almost trotting along when she was out and about in Aidensfield. It did not take long for me to realize that she was a regular sight in the village and was one of the local 'characters'.

Miss Hibbard lived in a large detached house overlooking the green; it was a splendid, if neglected, dwelling built in local moorland stone with a blue slate roof. It was constantly in need of a coat of paint and the garden was overgrown but I was to learn that the interior was full of antique furniture and a wonderful collection of rare Staffordshire pottery. In spite of her run-down appearance, Miss Hibbard was known to have a substantial private income and she could be very generous.

Although she rarely spent much money on herself, she did, from time to time, reveal flashes of true benevolence by donating cash to the church, to any village charity and to the Missions to Seamen or the Royal National Lifeboat Institution.

She was a very familiar figure in the village, pottering around the shops, going along to the church, visiting friends, helping at functions in the village hall or simply enjoying the fresh moorland air on long and lonely walks. But as she pottered about her business in Aidensfield, she began to intrigue me. I was first drawn to observing her after seeing her waiting for Arnold Merryweather's bus.

At ten o'clock one morning I was standing near the telephone kiosk, from where I could see the bus stop. Mabel Hibbard was standing there, empty basket in hand, as she waited for Arnold's service bus which would take her to Ashfordly. It was Friday: market day in Ashfordly.

There was no one else at the bus stop; other people would be going to town later or perhaps using their own cars. And so Mabel waited alone. As she waited, her eyes caught something in the window of the village shop. She pottered across a few yards of green to examine it. But as she started that manoeuvre, Arnold's bus appeared at the far end of Aidensfield, rising up the hill and heading for the bus stop. I felt sure Mabel would have seen or heard the oncoming bus, but she hadn't. I was too far away to shout at her, although I did try.

The bus rumbled past without halting and quickly disappeared around the corner as it made for Ashfordly. Mabel then returned to the bus stop, never realizing she'd missed it.

I decided to help. I drove to the bus stop in the police minivan and said, 'Hop in, Mabel, we can catch the bus.'

'Pardon?' she cupped an ear with her free hand.

'Bus!' I shouted. 'We can catch it.'

'No, it's not come yet,' she said. 'I'm waiting for it.'

'You've missed it,' I shouted again. 'When you were looking in the shop window; it came past and didn't stop. It's gone round the corner.'

'I never saw any bus,' she looked puzzled.

I realized that for the first time that she was as deaf as a proverbial post and went closer, shouting that if we hurried, we could catch Arnold's bus before it left the outskirts of Aidensfield.

It took some time for her to get the gist of my shouting and arm-waving and I know she was worried about getting into my police minivan, but I did catch the bus for her. With a cheery wave she boarded the rickety old vehicle and I saw the gigantic conductress, Hannah, come and take her fare.

From that time onwards, whenever I saw Mabel out and about in Aidensfield, I realized that she always missed seeing those things she wanted to see. She was always looking the wrong way at precisely the wrong moment.

One example occurred at the annual church fête. It was known that one of her nephews was a squadron leader in the RAF; he was a flying instructor at RAF Leeming and, as a special favour for the village, Mabel had been approached by the chairman of the organizing committee to ask her nephew if he could arrange a fly-past of jet aircraft while the fête was being held. Mabel had written to her nephew, Squadron Leader Hibbard, but he had stressed that it was impossible to make an official fly-past of jets for something as minor as Aidensfield church fête. He did say however, that, weather permitting, he would be in the air that day with five of his pupils in jet trainers, and he would arrange for them to fly over the village at 3 p.m. His own aircraft would make it six, and they would fly in formation, doing three runs over the village. It was all very unofficial, but the committee was delighted. They announced the flypast at 3 p.m. on all their publicity material and invited Mabel to be their guest of honour.

For the fly-past she would be seated on a platform with the vicar, the chairman, the doctor and other dignitaries. On the morning of the fête, Squadron Leader Hibbard telephoned his aunt to say that the weather was ideal for flying and that he would take to the air as planned, except that another commitment had arisen which meant that only one pass across Aidensfield was possible, not three as originally suggested. It meant that Aidensfield would still have its very own unofficial fly-past, however. There was great excitement about this event and it certainly attracted the crowds to the fête.

At a few minutes to three, therefore, a loudhailer announcement reminded the gathering of the impending arrival of six jet aircraft. Everyone assembled to wait. And then, in the distance across the moor, they could hear the distinctive sound of jet engines; Squadron Leader Hibbard had been true to his word and I saw the tiny outline of six distant aircraft as they flew ever so slowly towards the village.

It was at that precise moment, that Mabel decided to look in her handbag for a toffee. As she bent down to open her bag and rummage inside, I wanted to shout at her and tell her to look skywards but I was too far away and the crowd was shouting with happiness as they sighted the planes. Everyone else was looking at the sky; no one was bothering to observe Mabel except me. I was switching my gaze between Mabel and the oncoming aircraft.

It was almost as if I knew what was going to happen. Soon everyone was cheering as the six planes, in arrowhead pattern, swept across the moors. Mabel was oblivious to all this. Head down, she was rummaging in her bag while everyone else was gazing skywards – I continued to alternately look at her and at the planes, willing her to forget whatever she was seeking, but no one else was paying her the slightest attention. All eyes were on the heavens.

And then, with a roaring and whistling sound, the six shining aircraft, flying as slowly and as low as permissible, came directly over the church fête. They waggled their wings and flew on. Within seconds, they were disappearing over the horizon to the cheers of the crowd. I looked at Mabel.

Only then, as the jets whistled out of sight, did she find her toffee; she sat erect with a smile on her face, popped the sweet into her mouth and settled down to wait for her nephew. By then, of course, he was heading for the North Sea, never to return that day. She had neither seen nor heard the fly-past.

Everyone was so sorry that Mabel had missed the moment, but as I talked to people afterwards, I heard lots more similar tales about her. I was to learn, for example, that years earlier she had been invited to a friend's house to watch the Coronation on television, then a real national treat. Mabel was an ardent royalist and loved anything connected with the Royal Family. But seconds before the Archbishop of Canterbury had placed the crown on Her Majesty's head, Mabel had left the room to go to the toilet. When she'd returned, the supreme moment was over – and in those days there were no such things as video recorders to tape highlights from television.

Then, when she had watched a replay years later, she missed the crowning again because she dropped her spectacles on the floor at that precise moment and spent some minutes trying to find them. So far as anyone knew, Mabel had never actually seen Her Majesty being crowned – she had always been looking the other way whenever the ceremony had been repeated on television.

Some friends had tried to rectify those omissions when a local lass, Katherine Worsley of Hovingham, married the

Duke of Kent to become Her Royal Highness the Duchess of Kent. The date was 8 June 1961 and the entire population of the villages on the edge of the moors had become extremely excited. Her Majesty was a guest at the wedding and she would be driving through the countryside following the ceremony.

Locations and timings of Her Majesty's journey from Hovingham were publicized, so the people of Aidensfield felt they should take Mabel to a suitable position so that she would see the Queen. Having never seen a royal person in the flesh, Mabel had said she would cherish that moment for the rest of her life. To see the Queen in the flesh was like meeting God!

A small group of her friends had taken her to a knoll just outside Hovingham which was a superb vantage point. From there one could look along the road towards Hovingham and so gain a superb aspect of the royal cars as they sped towards us. Although this was before I became the village constable at Aidensfield, I was there too, on duty, because this was a busy road and there was a set of crossroads at which I had to halt all oncoming traffic to allow the royal procession to speed past. We knew the cars would be travelling at a very fast speed for security reasons and we would be warned, by police radio, when the royal motorcade left Hovingham Hall.

At that time, of course, I did not know Mabel, although in fact she would have been waiting within a few yards of my traffic duty position. And then we got word – the royal party was leaving; Her Majesty was to travel from Hovingham Hall to Malton to catch the royal train back to York and thence to London. That was my signal to halt all traffic at the crossroads. I shouted to the crowd that Her Majesty was en route, and would arrive in about five minutes. Everyone grew excited as I stood on the crossroads, ensuring an open run for the royal motorcade.

It was when I became village constable at Aidensfield that I heard about Mabel's mishap during her vigil. She had been among a crowd of friends and seconds before the royal cars appeared in the distance, Mabel decided she would have an orange.

She had brought some sandwiches, a flask of tea and an

orange to eat during the long wait. And, oblivious to the
cheers around her, she had ducked down to the grassy knoll
upon which she stood and had begun to ferret in her basket for
an orange. Then, having found one among the other picnic
paraphernalia, she had sought a knife with which to cut the
skin so she could peel it. And as she had squatted on her
haunches among the crowds, hunting for the knife, the
Queen's motorcade had flashed past at seventy miles an hour.
As Mabel had straightened up, orange in hand, the last police
car of the royal motorcade was heading out of sight. Mabel had
missed the Queen.

I did learn that there was a saying in the village that Miss
Mabel had missed again; she missed seeing the presentation of
the World Cup to Bobby Moore, captain of the winning
England soccer team in July 1966. She had just popped out to
make herself a cup of tea; she missed the thrilling sight of Neil
Armstrong stepping on to the moon in 1969, the first man to
do so, because she realized she'd forgotten to switch on her
oven to warm up so that she could cook herself a casserole.

Mabel's great love, however, was the church. A committed
Anglican, she thought God was an Englishman and believed
that the British Royal Family was somehow descended from
Him. Thus, for her, the Church of England with the British
Sovereign as its Supreme Governor was something founded
and approved of by God himself.

But being deaf she missed most of the points raised by the
Reverend Roger Clifton in his sermons. She also missed
advance information about church events such as parochial
parish council meetings, weddings, baptisms, confirmations
and funerals. None the less, she was a regular attender, relying
on the church notice board for times of special services,
additional functions and visits by the bishop.

It would take a long time to catalogue all the important
events that Mabel had managed to miss; she managed to miss
most of the local sights and occasions, and also contrived to
miss those of national interest which appeared on television.
And then one July, she died. She passed away very quickly
due to heart failure and so the time came for her own funeral.

The vicar of Aidensfield, the Reverend Roger Clifton, was

on holiday and his place had been taken for three weeks by the Reverent Austin Threadgill who hailed from Scotland. Six feet six inches tall, with a shock of black hair, he lived in the vicarage for those three weeks, and it was soon known that his strong point was his stentorian voice.

It was thunderous. Rumour was that he had been a sergeant-major in the war, but I have never heard such a powerful voice. It was deafening, even from a distance, and in the confines of the church it echoed about the building, reverberating from the walls and waking up the bats which slept in the belfry.

When the Reverend Threadgill opened up on Sunday mornings, his sermon could be heard by anyone walking past the church; I passed on one occasion when he was lecturing about sin, and his voice sounded like a clarion call to arms. His enunciation was clear though, and no one could avoid his message, nor could anyone go to sleep during his thunderclap sermons.

And, of course, Mabel had missed him. By dying when she did she had missed the only vicar whose voice she would have heard, but at least she had the honour of having this clamorous voice to conduct her funeral. The reverend's powerful and sonorous tones filled the church and brought tears to those who listened (probably because he was hurting their ear-drums), but Mabel did receive a loud and very fitting send-off.

Even at the graveside the roar of his words drowned the sound of passing traffic and we all felt that Mabel, wherever she was, would have heard him. Some said he had been sent by God especially to provide Mabel with a perfect end to her time on earth.

Later, though, a new bus stop was built in Aidensfield. It was right outside Mabel's old house. I wondered whether, if she had been alive, she would have missed the buses which came to that stop. Somehow, I think she would. I could envisage her standing there, waiting for Arnold's bus to appear and then, seconds before it arrived, hurrying back into the house for her purse.

Miss Mabel had gone through life missing things;

sometimes I wondered if that was why she had never married. Maybe she had missed every opportunity to fall in love, but actually, after she died, she was missed by everyone in Aidensfield.

★   ★   ★

Another busy lady, who never missed anything, was Mrs Fiona Tucker-Smith. Her husband worked away from home during the week, doing something mysterious but very financially rewarding in the City of London. He commuted to London from York station on Sunday nights and returned to Aidensfield on Friday evenings. While he earned his weekly crust in pin-stripe trousers and bowler hat he left Fiona to occupy herself during the week and so she did.

Her only source of interest outside her home was the church. She was a very tall and slim lady in her late forties who dressed in expensive but old-fashioned clothes, always of a dark colour but always immaculately kept. Her hair was pulled tightly back and she wore it in two ringlets curled around her ears where they looked like a cross between sea shells, curled-up fossil snakes and ear-muffs. Pale faced and devoid of make-up, she seldom smiled and tackled every aspect of life with the utmost severity and efficiency. A capable organizer, she did take part in many village events, particularly those which had a strong link with the Anglican parish church.

She spent her time raising funds for the parish, helping with the Remembrance Day distribution of red poppies, running raffles, coffee mornings, wine and cheese tastings and a host of other fairly upper-class functions, all of which were linked in some way with Aidensfield's Anglican parish church. She ignored the Catholic church in the village, even though some of the 'best' people in the village followed the ancient faith of this land, and she would not be caught dead in a bingo session, whist drive or beetle drive. Another character trait was that she tended to socialize only with people superior to herself. There were many such people in the district, some titled and others of aristocratic bearing, but she seemed able to distinguish between those whose money was 'new' and those whose ancestry could be traced in blue blood.

She ignored those with 'new' money, preferring to cultivate the local blue-bloods, even if they were impoverished. She was one of the villagers with whom I had a lot of official contact. This was because she was either chairman or secretary of all the parish church organizations (and in those days, chairmen were chairmen irrespective of sex, and they were not described as pieces of furniture, i.e. chairs). Fiona was chairman of the Parochial Church Council, chairman of the Church Fund-Raising Committee, secretary of the parish council, secretary of the Mothers' Union, secretary and president of the Womens' Institute, organizer of the rota for the church flower ladies, organizer of the rota for church cleaners, selector of hymns for Sunday services, compiler and typist for the parish magazine, organizer of sidesmen's duties, collector of Sunday collections and distributor of hymn books. She would also look after any official guests to the church, such as the bishop or visiting clergy, organizing coffee, lunch or tea for them.

She had not actually reached the stage of taking a service, administering communion or preaching the sermon, but she did tend the altar linen, polish the candlesticks and select the readings, both on Sundays and during the week.

The Reverend Roger Clifton seemed content to allow her this freedom. A charming bachelor, he was very busy because he ministered at several smaller neighbouring parishes and was a member of an ecumenical committee meeting at York. He did once indicate to me, off the record, that he allowed Fiona to undertake all these duties because she did fulfil some of the roles traditionally undertaken by the wife of a clergyman, but in addition he did feel sorry for her; her husband was away such a lot and she needed something to occupy her. For Fiona, the church in all its aspects provided some kind of fulfilment; she was in fact, a stand-in for the vicar's wife. And there is no doubt she did a very good job.

The snag was that none of the other willing and able ladies got a look in. Fiona kept them all at bay by ruling the committees and other organizations with remarkable efficiency, always being in charge and giving them menial tasks.

They wanted to feel useful, but in fact, they felt used. Throughout her work she used her considerable committee skills to keep the lesser ladies at a respectful and harmless distance. Fiona did everything; she even monitored the vicar's diary to ensure that he shared himself equally between his parishes, his duties for the York diocese and her village organizations.

But all good things come to an end and in this instance it happened with the transfer of Roger Clifton to an important post at York Minster. Clearly, his part-time church work in York had impressed those in authority. God, and the diocesan authorities, had more work for him and it seemed he was destined for a fine clerical career. The village was happy for him because he was such a charming and capable man, with a genuine love of his faith and respect for his congregation. Although the people of Aidensfield were sad to lose Roger, they were pleased for him. He had been a good, caring man of the church. Accompanying the news of his departure was a notice that his replacement would be a vicar from the Lake District with the unlikely name of the Reverend Christian Lord.

At this news the ladies of the parish scented dramatic changes because the Reverend Lord was married. Fiona might find herself thrust into a less prominent position, they hoped, and this might enable some of them to take more responsibility. They waited with considerable pleasure for the arrival of the new incumbent.

I was aware of all these manoeuvrings simply because I spent a lot of time in Aidensfield and, like the rest of the village, I wondered what was to befall Fiona. In due course, the Reverend and Mrs Christian Lord moved into the vicarage and, after allowing them a few days to settle in, I went to introduce myself as the village constable. Mrs Lord, a quietly spoken lady, was smothered in white emulsion and carrying a paint brush when she answered my knock. Though a headscarf protected some of her hair, I could see the rest was streaked with the emulsion. She looked very down-to-earth and practical and I found myself liking her.

'Sorry for the mess,' she beamed. 'But I thought I'd

brighten up this spot. I've got more on me than the walls! It's had a bachelor vicar living here, you can always tell. No flowers in the place, no bright colours, sombre wallpapers. I'm going to make the vicarage a bright and breezy place!'

That was good news and after I'd briefly introduced myself, she ushered me into the book-lined study where her husband was working on some papers. He stood up and shook my hand. I was quite surprised to see that he was a very small man, scarcely more than five feet two inches tall. He had a round, happy face and very thin fair hair on his head. He wore half-rimmed spectacles and peered over these as he greeted me.

'So God's law and man's law meet,' he laughed. 'You might be the inspiration for my first sermon, I need to make an impact. Sin and law-breaking ... now there's an idea.'

'Is it a sin to break the law?' I asked him. 'It is a sin to commit murder or theft, but is it a sin to ride a bike without lights or drink after time in the pub?'

'I might just take up those points,' he smiled. 'But let's get the important things settled first – has Ruth said anything about coffee?'

'Ruth will break off her decorating and organize coffee for the constable and the vicar!' sang a voice from outside the door.

'I don't know what I'd do without my wife,' he said with an infectious chuckle. 'How some vicars cope without wives I'll never know! I could never have been a Catholic priest, I just don't know who would have tidied my study and made my coffee.'

And so I introduced myself, making it known that I was a Catholic and therefore not one of his flock. We had a long, fun-laden talk about the village, its people, its environs, its problems and those in need. He listened intently, asking me lots of direct questions, and I came to the rapid conclusion that he would be an asset to Aidensfield. As I was about to take my leave, however, he indicated that I should stay a moment longer. 'I have one curious favour to ask,' he said.

'Fire away,' I invited.

'Have you come across a lady called Fiona Tucker-Smith?' he asked.

My response must have told him everything he wanted to

know because when I answered in a somewhat guarded way that I did know her, he said, 'I get the impression that she runs things around here? The church, I mean.'

'She is either secretary or chairman of every organization linked to your church,' I said.

'She's already trying to organize me,' he smiled. 'She's told me I'm to attend a wine and cheese party next Wednesday, that I must not fail to have one service a month for the Mothers' Union, that she will see to the prayer books, bell-ringing, flowers and church cleaners and that she will take care of my appointments diary.'

I decided I would explain to him the villagers' view of Fiona and so I did, saying that there were lots of other very capable and willing ladies who would love to become involved in village events. But Fiona had cornered the market.

'Thank you, Mr Rhea.'

'Nick,' I said. 'Everyone calls me Nick.'

'Nick, nick!' he chortled. 'I'll bet everybody says that?'

'I'm used to it,' I said.

'And me! Fancy my parents christening me Christian with a surname like Lord, and fancy me becoming a vicar! Sometimes when I'm leading prayers, I sound as if I'm calling my own name ... Is there any word from the Lord ... Lord be with you ... For thou Lord, art good and ready to forgive ... I could go on for ever! Anyway, back to Mrs Fiona What's-her-name.'

'She does mean well,' I said in her favour.

'I'm sure she does. But thank you for telling me about her. Ruth will take care of her, and she will do it in a most kind and gentle way. Ruth will see that the other ladies get their share of responsibility and take their part in helping Aidensfield church and its congregation.'

As I left, I had no idea how Mrs Lord would achieve the impossible, but within a month things began to happen. I was due to speak to the Mothers' Union about my work and on the morning of the event, I received a call from Fiona.

'Mr Rhea,' she said in her firm voice. 'When I booked you for this talk, I said I would be chairman for the evening and that I would introduce you to our members. Well, I have been asked to join a committee at Ashfordly, Lord Ashfordly is chairman, you know, it's a committee aimed at helping young people to appreciate the church. I am very honoured to be asked to serve his Lordship in this way, but it means I cannot chair your meeting. Both meetings are on the same night. Mrs Burley, the auctioneer's wife, is vice-chairman, and she will act for me at the Mothers' Union. I thought you ought to know.'

I thanked her for keeping me informed but, so far as I knew, this was the first time that Fiona had not fulfilled one of her many functions. When I arrived at the meeting, I found Mrs Burley firmly in the chair, with the vicar's wife at her side. After my talk, we had coffee and I managed to catch Ruth Lord for a few moments' talk. After the preliminaries, I found myself alone with her and made the comment, 'Fiona Tucker-Smith is attending another meeting?'

She smiled sweetly. 'I felt that a woman of her skills and determination had so much to offer and when I heard of a vacancy on Lord Ashfordly's committee, I felt it was perfect for her. And, Nick,' she smiled. 'I do know that the Archbishop is seeking someone to represent the diocese on the Church of England Children's Society, a most worthy charity. I have nominated Fiona for that too; they meet once a month in York. I did tell her that several past members of that committee have featured in the Queen's Birthday Honours lists ... I believe Fiona is very keen to become involved.'

'It would mean her giving up some of her local work?'

'It would indeed,' smiled Ruth Lord. 'And I'm sure we can find lots of capable replacements. I have a feeling we might need quite a lot.'

I smiled at her. She was a very pleasant lady and she was removing Fiona in a most graceful manner, and at the same time not dominating the organizations herself. This was the art of delegation; I felt that the Reverend and Mrs Lord would do the Lord's work at Aidensfield in a very acceptable way.

9   Faith, Hope and Charity

Man is by his constitution a religious animal.
Edmund Burke (1729–1797)

There is little doubt that the arrival of the Reverend Christian Lord and his admirable wife did result in an upsurge of interest in church matters at Aidensfield. The new vicar could preach an interesting and thought-provoking sermon, he had a sense of humour, he loved meeting the public and his wife soon began to take an active, but not domineering, part in the varied events of the village. Within a very short time the congregation at the Anglican parish church began to increase while the entire village welcomed the Reverend Lord and Mrs Lord to our peaceful rural community.

That is not to say that the previous vicar, Roger Clifton had been ineffective – he hadn't. Roger had been a very capable, kind and successful vicar and he had served Aidensfield as well as anyone could. He was right for that time. If anything, though, he lacked charisma; steady and reliable, he maintained a close and devoted following, but did not attract any new members of the faithful. His congregations were very static, comprising the same few each Sunday.

But in life, change is inevitable and the acceptance of change is important. The 1960s were times of great change, both in attitudes and in organizations in this country and overseas. The police service was changing and so was the church – and all change should be welcomed if it is harnessed for the good of the community. With Roger Clifton's departure, therefore, the Anglican parish was bound to experience changes and so it did.

The Catholic community of Aidensfield, of which I was part, also welcomed the new vicar; although the true spirit of ecumenism had not yet filtered to Aidensfield, it is fair to say that the Catholics and the Anglicans of Aidensfield and district did exist in mutual friendship even if they could not understand, or did not wish to understand, one another's long-held and cherished beliefs.

The older and more entrenched Anglicans continued to refer to the Catholics as Romans. They seemed to think we were foreigners or had some unwholesome allegiance to a foreign power. It seemed beyond their reasoning to credit Christ with having established a universal church which was not centred upon the United Kingdom – I'm sure some of them thought that Bethlehem and Jerusalem should really have been part of the British Empire. Those older Protestants never called us Catholics; they believed *they* belonged to the one, true Catholic church even though the law of England said the head of their church must be a Protestant.

The law also said that the head of the Church of England could never marry a Catholic. What the Protestants failed to realize was that the term 'Roman' Catholic did not come into use until the end of the sixteenth century – and then only in Britain. It is by no means a universal term. It seems to have been coined in England, a typically English means of implying there was something not quite English about the older, world-wide Catholic faith.

I was quite astonished to find that a lot of Anglicans had, and still have, no idea of the history of their own church, not knowing the drama and cruelty of the Reformation, not realizing that their church was not formed until the sixteenth century. There had been a church in England from the time of St Augustine's arrival in Canterbury in AD 596 – and he was a Catholic, having been sent by Pope Gregory I to convert the English. He was the first Archbishop of Canterbury, almost a thousand years before the Church of England was formed, the faith he brought came from God and from Rome. It was not the Church of England nor was it the Protestant faith. Augustine brought the church to England, he helped to establish the church *in* England, not the Church of England.

That church, with its new and protestant faith, was not established until 1559 – and it was then imposed on this country by the law of the land.

Thus the Church of England is less than 450 years old with no apostolic origins, it is state-controlled and paradoxically claims to be both Catholic and Protestant. It was members of that ancient Catholic church who built all those fine abbeys and churches which Henry VIII later crushed as he was trying to eradicate all evidence of the former church from this land.

Many of the faithful Anglicans of Aidensfield could not understand the ancient impact of English law upon their church – statutes such as the Acts of Supremacy and of Treason, laws by which Catholics who refused to accept the English sovereign as Supreme Head of the church were found guilty of treason and executed. The King, Henry VIII, declared himself head of the new Church of England; it was treason to deny him that office, and treason carried the death penalty. From the time of Henry VIII, therefore, the English sovereign would be head of the church, not the Pope, and as a consequence it was in January 1547 that King Edward VI became Supreme Head of the Church of England. He was nine years old at the time. Later Elizabeth I became the first female head of a church that is still fretting about the appointment of women priests.

In the centuries which followed, the law of England governed the new church in such a way that church and state became almost inextricably entwined. Even today, the Anglican church is governed by Parliament, which comprises people of many faiths or none at all. It seems strange that the British Parliament, through its laws, has any say in the running of God's church. To those outside the Church of England it seems an odd way to govern a church.

The Catholics, on the other hand, viewed the Anglicans with some suspicion, blaming them for the destruction of all their medieval monasteries and abbeys, for seizing all their finest churches, for taking over their lands and executing their leaders. But it wasn't the Anglican church leaders who did these things; it was the state, although by then church and state were as one.

With the loss of their lands and church buildings, denied the right to practise their faith from the time of the Reformation, the Catholics went into hiding for more than a couple of centuries. In spite of the risks to their lives, many men did become priests, returning in secret to spread the gospel. So the old Catholic religion survived, often in secret and often at risk of a cruel death to those who practised it. In spite of their treatment, Catholics remained true to their country and to their church, but could not accept that the British sovereign was head of their religion. They did accept him as head of their country, but not of their church.

With the passage of some 270 years, Catholics eventually regained some of their old lost rights through the Catholic Emancipation Act of 1829. This restored the rights of Catholics to sit in Parliament, to inherit land, to join HM Forces, to act as judges and to enjoy a university education. Those and more rights had been denied them since the Reformation, but even now no Catholic can become Prime Minister nor can the British sovereign be a Catholic. If a member of the Royal Family marries a Catholic, then he or she forfeits all rights to the succession. I don't think the same stricture applies if the sovereign marries a member of any other faith or even an atheist. So, even in the 1990s, there are still restrictions upon Catholics in Britain; religious bias still exists in our fine country. But even if the constitution of Britain continues to be discriminatory in matters of religion, most of the people either do not care or prefer to ignore those old divisions.

For some of the people of Aidensfield, though, those old divisions did cause hurt and anger, and from time to time ancient prejudices did surface. In spite of an outward attitude of tolerance between the faiths, there were still undercurrents which had roots in the badly-named 'Reformation' which had occurred more than 430 years earlier.

On one occasion, there was a fight outside a dance hall and I found myself having to sort out something which had all the appearances of an unprovoked attack upon a young man.

The assailant was a powerful farmer called Jack MacKay and he had a pretty daughter of seventeen. She was called

Rebecca and she had attended a dance in Elsinby village hall. Jack had driven her to the hall at eight o'clock and had said he would return at 11.45 p.m. to collect her. I was on duty outside the hall, as was my normal practice on dance nights, when I heard a commotion. It was just after 11.45 p.m. and the dancers were leaving, many of them in pairs. Some had been established as couples long before the dance started but other pairings had been formed only that evening. New romances were blossoming, I felt; this was not surprising, of course, because village dances were one of the places where the young people of Aidensfield and district met and fell in love.

My attention was drawn to the fracas by a lot of shouting and cursing; it was in the car park beside the hall and as I turned to investigate the disturbance, somebody shouted, 'Mr Rhea, there's a fight near the gate!'

I ran across the car park in the darkness to find two men scuffling and shouting; the younger one was clearly on the defensive and his older, larger assailant was shouting abuse before a curious gathering of friends who tried to separate them. I waded in, shouting 'Police', and managed to seize the collar of one assailant. I hauled him backwards, the tightness of his collar restricting his breathing and so forcing him to break his hold on the other.

I found I'd got in my grip a man in his early forties, not a youth in his teens as I might have expected. I recognized him as Jack MacKay, a farmer from Elsinby. The other fighter was much younger, probably in his late teens or early twenties. He was Gerry O'Connell, the son of an electricity board worker from Aidensfield.

'Now just calm down, the pair of you,' I shouted.

'He just came for me,' the younger man was straightening his clothes and tidying his hair. 'I never said a word ... the man's crazy ... he just lashed out!'

And it was only then that I saw Rebecca in the background, biting her lip as she suddenly found herself a reluctant focus of attention in this strange affair.

'What's all this about, Jack?' I asked the older man.

'I'm having no Papist courting my lass,' he said in a strong

Scots accent. 'I want no Romish offspring near me, no Papist trash in my family ...'

'I'm a Papist,' I said quietly. 'But I'm sure that young man isn't trash. Catholic, yes, trash no.'

'He called me that,' said the youngster, licking his lips where Jack's first blow had landed. 'I don't know what's got to him.'

Jack belonged to a fiery Scots religion, one of the so-called Wee Frees, and I'd long known of his religious intolerance. He was a very charming man otherwise, a good farmer and a successful businessman, but his deep religious bias could surface at the most awkward moments. And when he'd seen his daughter kissing a Catholic 'good-night' outside the dance hall, he'd been unable to restrain himself. 'Love thy neighbour as thyself' was not a commandment which was accepted by members of his church; they hated Catholics and made no secret of it, in spite of calling themselves Christians.

'Jack, calm down or you'll be arrested,' I bellowed at him to rouse him from his fanatical stupor.

My voice so very close to his ear seemed to do the trick and he suddenly relaxed, as if all his anger had evaporated.

'Sorry, Nick,' quite suddenly he was as calm and rational as ever. 'Sorry, I didn't mean to do that ... it's just that ...'

'Jack, you've got to learn to control this dislike of Catholics. I'm a Catholic but I don't go around clouting members of the Scottish Free Churches ... and I don't go around arresting them without good cause.'

'He was kissing my daughter.'

'Is that a crime? Would Christ have reacted like you did? For most of the time, you live a good Christian life, Jack, I know that – no alcohol, prayers on Sundays, no swearing ... yet you blow up like this!'

'It's those Papists ...'

'Look, I suggest you shake hands with young Gerry and then we can forget this. I'm sure he wouldn't want me to prosecute you for assaulting him, the press would have a field day with this story, you know – religious strife in Elsinby!'

'I can never shake hands with a Papist,' he said.

'If I was St Peter, would you shake hands with me?'

'Aye, of course, Peter was a good man.'

'He was the first Pope,' I said. 'That's not religious dogma, it's part of world history. And he was appointed to the job by Christ himself, even your Bible will tell you that! Thou are Peter and upon this rock I will build my church ... you've heard the words, surely?'

'You're playing with words, Mr Rhea.'

'And you're playing with fire, Jack. Hell fire, I shouldn't be surprised.'

At this point, Rebecca came forward and took her father's arm. 'Come along, dad, take me home.'

He looked at Rebecca, then at me, then at the crowd which had gathered and nodded, 'Aye, right,' was all he said. He did not apologize for his actions and I decided to let him go rather than inflame the situation any further. There was absolutely no point in arresting him or bringing about a prosecution – it would serve no useful purpose at all. As I made my decision, he turned his back on Gerry O'Connell and walked away without a word. Rebecca trotted after him.

'You'll not press charges, Mr Rhea?' said Gerry as he came over to me, still nursing his jaw with his hand.

'No,' I said. 'But next time you fancy the daughter of one of the Wee Frees of Scotland, make sure her dad's not around to see you in action!'

'I've been seeing her a while,' said the lad. 'She never said anything about her dad being likely to blow up like that.'

'She knows you're a Catholic?' I asked.

'Yes, we often have talks about religion, she's very interested in my church, she says her mum wanted to leave Scotland to get away from the influence of the Wee Frees, to gain a wider perspective, she said. But her dad won't give up.'

'Give him time,' I said. 'If he was brought up in that mould, he'll never shake off the shackles. It's up to you to show the Jack MacKays of this world that Catholics haven't got forked tails, that the Pope isn't an Antichrist, and that we are all human beings with a love of God.'

'It's not easy, coping with a man like that,' he said. 'I'll be scared even to let him see me with Rebecca, he might turn violent again.'

'Just don't give him chance, and don't react the same way as him,' I advised. 'Keep calm – in fact, you made a very good start tonight. You could have flattened him, I'd guess.'

'If you hadn't turned up, I reckon I could have floored him,' grinned Gerry. 'I was my school boxing champion, I can use my fists.'

And so the drama was over. Gerry walked home without his girlfriend, while Rebecca drove her father back to his farm. Later, I saw Gerry and Rebecca going for walks together on the moors or visiting Strensford or the coastal villages, but whenever I met them I never referred to that incident.

Several years later, Rebecca did marry Gerry; they married in Elsinby Catholic church before a happy gathering of friends and family. The only man missing was Jack MacKay. He died three weeks before the wedding; some said his death was an act of God. I wondered if it was from a broken heart.

* * *

I think a lot of people are interested in religion, probably out of curiosity; many who never go near a church or attend a service frequently express their views on religion in a manner which shows they often think about it. I knew a man who claimed to be an atheist; he had no belief whatsoever in God or divinity, and yet he peppered his conversation with phrases like, 'God willing', 'God only knows' and 'God help me'.

Another such character was Geoffrey Ditchburn, a retired chemical worker. He found religion something of a puzzle and often tried to rationalize his thoughts in conversations with those who attended church.

He'd worked all his life in the chemical industry on Teesside, being an expert on man-made fibres, and he retired to a life of rural bliss in Aidensfield. During my patrols I would often see him out for a brisk walk with his two labradors, Bill and Ben. Geoffrey, a rounded, cheerful-looking man with a bald head and tiny ears, walked swiftly with the aid of a walking stick. He spent hours roaming the moors and woods looking for unusual insects. Whenever he saw me, however, he would stop for a chat and he did have a tremendously wide knowledge of politics and world affairs; he also had a wonderful sense of humour. It was due to the arrival of the Reverend Lord that, one day when he met me on the village green, his topic of conversation was the church. After the usual pleasantries, he asked if I had met the new vicar.

'Yes,' I said. 'Several times,' and I followed by expressing a favourable opinion of Christian Lord.

'I never go to church,' he said solemnly. 'I can say my prayers whenever and wherever I want; I don't need pews and walls and incense and colourful robes to help me meet God.'

'You believe in God?' I asked.

'Yes, although not necessarily in the form of a bad-tempered old man sitting on a throne and delegating responsibility to St Peter. We all know St Peter finished up as nothing more than a heavenly bouncer, deciding who comes into heaven and who doesn't. What a job – it must be worse than being a bouncer at a night-club, having to make all those decisions. And he won't get paid either. Imagine being faced with villains – Hitler or Stalin or Henry VIII – would you have let any of that lot into heaven? Remember, once they're in, you can't turf them out again; it's worse than a night-club, at least at a night-club you can get rid of unwanted guests. And suppose Peter refused to let somebody in, and God said he was wrong? I mean, Peter might not have admitted Martin Luther but God might have thought he was a decent chap. There again, Peter might have admitted William the Conqueror but God might not have wanted him even though he was a Catholic who built lots of churches and abbeys; God might have been frightened he would try to take over the entire kingdom of heaven and besides, not everybody likes Norman architecture. Then there was Hannibal and all his elephants to look after; do you reckon St Peter wanted him in heaven with all those elephants? I mean, you can't just assume that whatever Peter wanted God would agree to, and nobody wants their boss altering their decisions ...'

'I'd never looked at it like that,' I had to admit. 'Do you always see religion like this?'

'I think I see it logically,' he smiled. 'I often believe there were politicians in the universe long before God created the world.'

'How on earth do you come to that conclusion?' I asked.

'Well, the Old Testament says God created the world out of chaos, and politicians always cause chaos!' he grinned.

I chuckled at this view, but he went on, 'So what about Noah's Ark?'

'What about it?' I responded.

'Well, with all those animals on board in such a small place, and on wooden boards. If animals pee or crap on wood, it raises one hell of a stink. So what about that stink? You can't wash it away, it lingers for months with just one dropping, so can you imagine what it would be like after months of droppings from every one of those animals and birds! God, the thought is appalling! There were no air fresheners in those days, you know, and posies of violets wouldn't be much of a help. You imagine having all those wild creatures on board, all needing to be fed and watered and mucked out. Who did all that? I can't believe that yarn about Noah and the Ark, nobody could tolerate that stink all that time! There's no wonder the bloody dove left, is there?'

I had to chuckle at the picture his words produced in my mind, then he went on.

'I often think of the church as a football team,' he said. 'Every church I mean, not just the Catholics or the Protestants or Aidensfield church.'

'A football team?' I was puzzled.

'Yes. Think of a football as containing all the sins of the world. Now God doesn't want it in heaven, does he? He doesn't want all those sins being kicked about in heaven, so the goal is heaven.'

'And the devil's the striker?'

'Yes, the devil is the other side – he's trying to get sin into heaven. God wants to stop him.'

'So you see God as the goalkeeper?' I asked.

'Got it in one!' he beamed. 'God is there trying to keep sin out of heaven, but it's a tough job, so he needs help. That's who the other team members are. The Pope is the centre forward and the others in the front line are the outside left and outside right, and inside left and inside right, depending on the opinions of the cardinals. Left wingers and right wingers.'

'So the half backs?' I asked. 'Centre half?'

'The Orthodox churches,' he said. 'Greek Orthodox, Eastern Orthodox and Russian Orthodox. Centre half, left half and right half.'

'And the backs? Left and right full backs?'

'Church of England on the right, other Protestants on the left. They're there in case all else fails. And when they're in play, they all kick the ball to one another; all the churches are trying to pass the blame for sin to one another, aren't they? If sin gets past any of them, then it's up to God to become the goalie and stop it from reaching heaven.'

'But in a real football match a lot of goals are scored,' I put to him.

'And I reckon the devil gets a lot of sinful folks into heaven,' he grinned. 'Including a lot of churchmen and women.'

'So where does the ref come into your scheme of things?' I asked.

'St Peter,' he said. 'He's the ref and the apostles are linesmen, all working to reach decisions about what's fair and what isn't, what's sinful and what isn't. I mean, a lot of fouls are committed in the name of religion.'

'And some goals are not counted due to the off-side rule,' I added.

'Some things which are not sins now might have been sins in the past, like sex before marriage,' he said.

'I suppose, in your scheme of things, countries who fight battles in the name of religion also commit fouls?' I said.

'Got it,' he grinned. 'So you see, Nick, I can't really take religion seriously. Every time I hear a priest or vicar preaching I think he's a commentator at a football match. I finish up wondering which side will win.'

'I wonder if God does the football pools?' I asked him.

'The thing that worries me,' he grinned, 'are the spectators. I often wonder which team they want to win!'

★   ★   ★

One of the innovations from the new vicar was the venue of the harvest festival.

He decided to hold it in the pub instead of the parish church, one reason being that all members of the community, irrespective of their religious persuasion, could attend.

He had a word with the Catholic priest, Father Adrian, who felt it was a superb idea, although the Methodist minister, Pastor Smith, felt that the alcohol being served might detract from the solemnity of the occasion. Anything more than a glass of dry sherry was, in the views of some of his parishioners, rather sinful, even if the fruit of the vine did feature strongly in many church services. In spite of his reservations, however, he did agree to participate after Father Adrian reminded him that Christ was born in an inn and that he later produced some very good wine for the wedding at Cana, his very first miracle. Clearly, added the Reverend Lord, Jesus was not against a moderate tipple.

The inn's harvest festival was probably the first truly ecumenical service in the district. It raised one question though – if this was to be a joint service, should the Catholics and Methodists go ahead with their own normal services, or should this be the *Aidensfield* harvest festival rather than the Anglican parish harvest festival? Decisions would have to be made, in parochial church council of course.

Meanwhile George Ward, the landlord, was delighted and readily gave his consent. He even said he would not charge a fee for the use of his premises. A large attendance was expected, so the service would have to be held in the bar because there was no other suitable room at the inn. The only consideration that George requested was that the regulars were not barred from their own pews in the bar.

Christian Lord said, 'That's the whole idea, George. We want everybody there, pub faithful and church regulars. This will be one way of getting people to a church service who would never normally venture through my doors.'

'Like Claude Jeremiah Greengrass?' smiled George.

'And others, like you,' beamed the genial vicar. 'Now, as you know, the congregation always bring samples of their produce for display in church during the harvest festival – vegetables, fruit, cereals, potatoes and so forth, and when the festival is over, we donate those offerings to charity.'

'Yes, a very nice idea,' George agreed.

'Well, in my view,' said the vicar, 'few charities need fruit and vegetables these days. They're more in need of funds. They need money for furniture, premises, equipment, maintenance and so forth, so on this occasion, I propose holding an auction of the produce after the service. In your pub, I might add. I believe we shall raise a lot of money which we can donate to a worthwhile charity or charities.'

'It sounds a great idea,' enthused George. And so the vicar's plans were put into action. In due course he selected his date, in October, and the announcement was made. Notices were printed and distributed around the village and they asked for the faithful to bring their fruit and vegetables to decorate the pub instead of the church. In the meantime, the Catholics and the Methodists decided not to hold their own harvest festivals this year. Instead, they would all join the village harvest festival in the pub. There were some objections, as all the clergymen had expected, but it was hoped that the objectors would reconsider their decisions for next year.

The produce flooded in. George was overwhelmed with cabbages, carrots and broccoli, corn dollies, jars of strawberry jam and scrubbed potatoes of massive dimensions. In the week before the festival the pub's appearance changed to resemble that of a fruit and vegetable stall. There were apples on his optics, rhubarb behind the till and celery in the lager glasses. Mushrooms filled ash trays, plums adorned the domino boards and sprigs of mint decorated the dart board.

Ladies of all religious persuasions came to arrange the produce in the most tasteful manner and, it is rumoured, even Miss Wisdom, the chapel caretaker, sampled one of George's free sherries. Preparation for the festival was a jolly occasion in itself, and then the great night arrived.

The first noticeable fact was that the wives of the pub regulars turned up; the effect of this was to double immediately the number of early customers in the bar. Some of their older children came too because their mums and dads felt that, if mum was going to the pub, then so could Johnny and Jenny. Thus the evening was already guaranteed to be a success. George was beginning to think it was his lucky night and that his foresight in appointing two extra bar staff for the night had been wise.

Claude Jeramiah Greengrass turned up too, with Alfred on a lead and with an offering of parsnips tied to his collar. Then the church congregations began to arrive, accompanied by relations and friends. The pub-shy Methodists crept into this sinful place with eyes wide as they sought signs of the devil; the Anglicans came with slightly more bravado, while for most of the Catholics the pub was a regular haunt. Many of them came here on Sunday mornings straight after Mass. But on this night, the choirs came too and to avoid arguments as to who should play the pub piano during the service, (Anglican, Methodist or Catholic?), George said he would do so.

I was there, in uniform, to keep order should this crowd become over-enthusiastic for the fruit of the vine or the ears of the barley field, but there was no trouble. It was a most friendly and good-humoured occasion. The joint service, with the lovely, practised voices of the Methodists leading the singing, was a joy; everyone joined in. Even Alfred raised his voice to the heavens when the singers reached the higher notes, his lone wolf-like howling adding a touch of melancholy to 'We plough the fields and scatter', and also in 'Come to God's own temple, come; Raise the song of harvest-home!' Alfred's greatest moment, however, was in his accompaniment to 'All things bright and beautiful, all creatures great and small'.

When the singing was over and sore throats had been eased with several drops of George's finest ale, tomato juice, vodka, soft drinks, whisky with green ginger or other throat-relieving potions, it was time for the auction. The auctioneer was Rudolph Burley, whose fine bass voice could be heard over any other human din. After suggesting that the congregation gather in to their bosoms yet another drink or two to keep them going 'Ere winter storms begin', he began his auction of the vegetable produce. The resultant income would be equally divided between the three denominations represented here, and they could then allocate the monies to the charities of their choice.

With apples being knocked down for ten times their normal

price, farmers buying back their own potatoes and beetroot, and jars of jam raising the cost of a meal of caviare, it was a very successful occasion. Well over £175 was raised, a large sum in those days, and everyone felt it was a success. Even Pastor Smith, with two malt whiskies, a pint of best bitter and a brandy beneath his belt, was beginning to appreciate the merits of singing hymns in a pub. Claude's parsnips raised three shillings and some of my raspberries fetched half a crown.

The evening concluded with a famous harvest hymn but I'm sure that I heard George mispronounce one word. The harvest hymn 'To thee, O Lord, our hearts we raise' contains the line 'The hills with joy are ringing'. As the massed choirs of Aidensfield raised the pub roof with their voices in a grand finale, and as Alfred's dulcet tones drowned the accompanying piano music, I was sure I heard George's fine voice singing, 'The tills with joy are ringing.'

10   All Change

Fear of change perplexes monarchs.
John Milton (1608–1674)

If the fear of change perplexed monarchs, then it most certainly perplexed police officers, especially those serving in the 1960s. In the years immediately following the turmoil of the Second World War, police forces had settled into a cosy routine laced with mutual respect between themselves and the public. They were quite content to potter along in their comfortable, old-fashioned way. Police officers had no false notions of their place in society – they sought not wealth but a means of providing an efficient if sometimes out-moded service to those by whom they were paid.

Modern contraptions like personal radio sets had not yet reached the rural beats – there is a tale of one sergeant being issued with twenty brand new radio sets for his officers whereupon he promptly locked them in a cupboard, saying to his men, 'These things are too expensive and too good for you to use.' Bicycles were quite suitable for patrol work, feet were even better, and if a constable wished to go somewhere at high speed he would commandeer a passing car or jump on to a bus. Ordinary constables were not expected to use cars and most certainly they were not expected to own a motor car.

In that leisurely era, crime fighting and crime prevention was done at a rather gentle pace. It is not surprising that there was some resistance to constables driving cars while on duty – hitherto, the method of patrolling a town beat had been restricted to a pair of whopping size elevens, although rural constables did have motor cycles and eventually minivans. But their town colleagues had to plod around the streets without a thought of the current concern about Incident Response Times, while motor vehicles were used almost exclusively by exalted ranks like sergeants, inspectors and superintendents. In the minds of those in authority over constables, there was something almost obscene in a constable actually being allowed to drive a police car, unless he was a member of the élite Road Traffic Division. Certainly ownership of a motor car by a constable was treated with some suspicion – questions were asked, such as where did he get the money to run a car? How can a constable afford such a luxury? And most certainly, police houses were never equipped with garages for one's private car.

As the 1960s progressed, however, police constables could afford to buy motor cars, and this coincided with rumours of massive changes within the police service. Sergeant Blaketon had already had a whiff of change, but that whiff was soon to turn into a gale of impressive power. The oncoming changes were not contained in the proverbial breath of fresh air – they were to be borne upon typhoon-style gusts.

For example, new ranks were being created – there was to be a new rank of chief inspector (between inspector and superintendent) and another new rank of chief superintendent which would be higher than a superintendent. In addition, a rank of deputy chief constable would be created and this would be higher than the existing assistant chief constable. With the arrival of a deputy chief constable, there would be two assistant chief constables who would function at a lower level, one being responsible for the administration of the force and the other supervising operational matters. To cater for this influx of senior officers police divisions were to be enlarged to accommodate the new chiefs and to give them something useful to do, and so the new top brass would be able to spend more days driving around in expensive cars with a sense of importance. In the terminology of the force at that time, the changes meant there were going to be far more chiefs than Indians.

With these rumoured (and eventually imposed) developments, rural beats were to be enlarged with inevitable change to the boundaries of sections and sub-divisions. There would be fewer sections, sub-divisions and divisions, but the new ones would be far larger than the old. It was probably the advent of motorized constables that was the basis for these changes.

There was no doubt that these developments, when they arrived, would affect rural beats like Aidensfield. The village constable (me, in other words) would, if the rumours were correct, be expected to operate in areas previously covered by neighbouring constables. Rural constables might even be drafted into the local towns to perform duties – not a very nice prospect. That notion was even worse for sergeants like poor old Blaketon – if he was ordered to patrol the streets of a town he would be subservient to the local hierarchy, not king of his own midden as he was at Ashfordly. There is little wonder that these moves were resisted, if only for personal reasons. It could be argued that they were necessary for the efficiency of the force and our service to the public but the personal trauma they created might even be counter-productive. Good man-management was not a strong feature of the service at that time – we simply obeyed orders.

If the trend towards wholescale modernization was adopted, then some rural police houses would close and be sold, their occupants being moved into town for routine patrol duties. Areas hitherto policed by, say, three or four constables could now be made the responsibility of only one. In some cases, it was rumoured, village constables would work as a team, three or four of them covering an increased area in a motor vehicle and having their day's duty divided into three eight-hour shifts. In this way the rural bobby, with his twenty-four hour responsibility for a handful of small communities, would disappear. Instead, he would work eight-hour shifts, like a town officer, but over a wider patch with more villages. His colleagues would work similar shifts, thus ensuring that all communities, however small, were served twenty-four hours a day by a motor car containing a police officer. That's how the theory was explained but the system rarely worked in practice because one constable can only be in one place at any one time. If he was dealing with a traffic accident on the outskirts of

Ashfordly, he could not be expected to supervise the pub at Elsinby.

I could see that the public would begin to believe there were fewer police officers, and indeed these projected changes did mean that a rural constable's proud commitment to his very own rural beat would be reduced or even eliminated.

But perhaps the most awesome and threatening of all these rumoured changes was that police forces themselves were to be altered. During the 1960s the Boundary Commission was in the throes of examining the geography of the British counties, county boroughs and cities with a view to reshaping them. It was said that city police forces like York, Leeds and Hull would vanish upon being absorbed by their neighbouring counties. The counties themselves would change too, with the famous Yorkshire Ridings being abolished in favour of new counties with names like North Yorkshire, West Yorkshire, South Yorkshire, Humberside and Cleveland.

The East Riding of Yorkshire would vanish without trace, becoming the northern part of Humberside. Rumours of this kind of 'progress' produced horror stories among police officers who realized that if new counties were created with their new county councils and new police authorities, then new police forces would also be formed. There would be new procedures, new bosses, new demands and lots of new problems.

During my time at Aidenfield, however, all these changes were little more than rumours but some rumours have a habit of becoming fact. It is fair to say that many of us did worry about our jobs because the amalgamation of police forces would inevitably mean that some top jobs would be lost. And if the top jobs were lost, then the chances of promotion were reduced. For example, if three police forces were merged to become only one, then at least two chief constables would lose their posts. The same would apply to the lower ranks but none of us felt this would affect mere constables. Any police force could function without superintendents but none could function without the humble constables on the beat.

But if the authorized establishment of a new police force was, say, 1,500 constables and the amalgamated constituent forces between them had 1,700 constables, then two hundred constables would have to disappear. Admittedly, this would be done by natural wastage such as retirements or resignations, so there would be no redundancies or sackings.

None the less, I do know that the constant rumours about such far-reaching changes did create a cloud of worry among a lot of officers, old and young, in high ranks and low ranks, in town and country. Another of the horrors awaiting officers in ancient cities was that they would have to patrol rural areas and deal with ghastly things like swine fever, sheep pox, epizootic lymphangitis, glanders or farcy. These were all diseases of animals, something of a problem for a city-bred officer who couldn't distinguish a pheasant from a ferret or a Friesian. And to patrol a lonely moorland road at night, without the benefit of street lighting and with an owl hooting in the distance, was something not relished by townie constables.

While long-serving officers like Sergeant Blaketon were fretting about their careers due to these threatened changes, young whizz-kids like Inspector Pollock were not. The highly educated, police college trained Pollocks of the police service saw themselves as the new wave of senior officers; they regarded themselves as the chosen few, men charged with the duty of modernizing a stagnating service and bringing to it all the techniques and skills of those trained in skilled man-management and organizational efficiency. Pollock saw himself as a future chief constable in a most modern and efficient police force; in fact, he saw himself as something of a saviour to the public he had sworn to serve.

I felt he would never achieve very senior rank because he was something of a twit; one of his failings was that he could never remember the names of his subordinates. This became apparent to me when, for some reason, he began to call me PC MacTavish.

This was something of a departure from the normal. Many senior officers referred to constables by their surnames – I was just Rhea. The force was full of Smiths, Jones, Browns and Greens in addition to some more colourful names like Fox, Hare and Fowler, Martin, Swift and Swallow to name but a few. But, as constables, they were known by their surnames to all ranks higher than their own. Sergeants and above called constables by their surnames. Sergeants were addressed as sergeant by all ranks, while inspectors and all higher ranks were called sir by their subordinates.

In some smaller forces, however, particularly in cities and boroughs, the constables were known by the numbers they wore upon their uniforms. Thus PC 6 Brown would be known simply as 'Six'. One would therefore receive messages like 'What duty is Six working this weekend?' or 'Has Six been seen since 9 a.m?' This was even carried into off-duty periods so that news came along that Six was getting married, or his wife had had a child or that Six was sick with influenza. I've attended many social functions where officers called each other by their official numbers; quite literally, therefore, some officers were mere numbers in their force. Some police officers went through their entire service not knowing the real identity of Six or Ten or Ninety-Nine. In similar vein, one of the best known fictional police constables just after the Second World War was widely known to the public as simply PC 49.

Some recruiting officers had great fun allocating numbers to police officers – we had a PC Walls who was given the number 4, one called Fawcett who was given 444, another called Goode who was given number 2, one called Green who was given number 10 and one called Steeples who was given the number 200.

Thus we had Four Walls; Four, Four, Four Fawcett; Two Goode, Ten Green (who was nicknamed Ten Green Bottles) and Two Hundred Steeples as members of our constabulary. I was the very ordinary PC 575 Rhea. Later, when the police forces did amalgamate, one unfortunate officer was given the number 999 – his name was Ward. Thus he became known as Emergency Ward and another, with the number 1001, became known as the Carpet Cleaner because of a popular advert for a fluid known as 1001. The advertisement, sung to a jingle, said that you could clean a big, big carpet for less than half a crown. That is 12½p in modern money.

To be called by someone else's name, however, was somewhat unusual, even by police standards. It was especially unusual if this was done by one's local inspector. I had met our new senior officer, Inspector Pollock, on several occasions whilst I was at Aidensfield and in each case he had addressed me as either Rhea or PC Rhea.

But one Saturday evening I was patrolling Ashfordly during a shortage of officers when Inspector Pollock arrived by car. He climbed out, as smart as ever, and I saluted him.

'Good evening, PC MacTavish,' he said. 'All in order?'

'Yes, sir, all correct,' I informed him, wondering if I had heard the name MacTavish or whether I had misunderstood some other word or phrase. I did not correct his error on that first occasion and he joined me in a short patrol around the streets with me indicating pubs where trouble might spill on to the Saturday night streets. He asked me several questions about the town, its local people and problem areas, and I got the impression he was quizzing me about my knowledge of Ashfordly.

He spent about fifteen minutes with me before departing. As he was leaving I slung up a departing salute and he said, 'Carry on, PC MacTavish.'

'I'm PC Rhea, sir,' I corrected him as he was entering his car, but he didn't hear me as he drove away. I puzzled over his error but thought little more about it until I was on early morning patrol about a week later. I had to make a tour of my own beat, in my minivan, between 6 a.m. and 9 a.m., making points outside the telephone kiosks of Elsinby at 7 a.m. and Briggsby at 8 a.m. These were check points in case anyone wanted to contact; it was a daft system because I had a police radio fitted to my vehicle. Through it, I was in constant contact with my sectional, divisional and headquarters offices.

However, as I was standing outside the kiosk in Elsinby, Inspector Pollock hove to in his smart official car. He climbed out, slung up a salute and asked, 'All correct, PC MacTavish?'

'It's PC Rhea, sir,' I told him.

'Really, where?' he asked, turning around to seek PC Rhea.

'No, sir, I'm PC Rhea,' I sighed. 'I'm not PC MacTavish; you called me MacTavish!'

'Did I really? But you are MacTavish, surely?'

'No, sir, I'm PC Rhea.'

'Are you sure?'

'Very sure, sir. Rhea is my surname, I've never been called MacTavish.'

'Oh, well, sorry about that. You do look like MacTavish, though. Remarkable. A most remarkable likeness. You could be brothers, twins even. Astonishing.'

'I'm afraid I don't know a PC MacTavish, sir,' I had to admit.

'So you are Rhea! Well, well, fancy me not recognizing you. You're the Aidensfield constable, aren't you?'

'Yes, sir.'

'Then where is PC MacTavish stationed? Why did I mistake you for MacTavish? Tell me that.'

'I don't know, sir, perhaps he's new to the area.'

'Of course! That's it! A new arrival, he's been with us a couple of months, a probationer constable, straight from training school. PC Alastair MacKenzie MacTavish, a Scotsman.'

'Really, sir?'

'He's stationed at Strensford. But my goodness, Rhea does look like you, MacTavish ...'

'Rhea, sir.'

'Who?'

'Me, sir. I'm Rhea.'

'My goodness, so you are.'

'MacTavish is the other one, sir.'

'Yes, you're right, of course. You really are both so alike, it's incredible. Now, how's things otherwise?'

'Very quiet this morning, sir, no problems.'

And so, after chatting to me for about ten minutes, off he went. I felt he'd left in a cloud of utter confusion but was sure that assertion of my identity, uncertain though it had been, would establish my name in his mind. I was wrong. Whenever he met me in Aidensfield village, or at my police house, he called me PC Rhea, but whenever I encountered him away from Aidensfield, he always called me PC MacTavish.

As this absurdity continued, I decided to find out a little more of PC Alastair MacKenzie MacTavish of Strensford Police. From friends stationed there, I discovered he was a new recruit with a strong Scots accent, but that he was indeed about my height and had my colouring. Furthermore, one of my friends did say he had a partial resemblance to me and, like Pollock, did state we might be taken for brothers. But the most distinctive difference was MacTavish's voice – he had a very pronounced Scots accent while I spoke with a distinct Yorkshire voice.

It was inevitable that I should meet MacTavish and our first meeting occurred when we were both selected for duty at Redcar Races. This was one of our regular and enjoyable extra duties; every one of us looked forward to duty at one or more of the local racecourses.

In the 1960s, the North Riding Constabulary was responsible for policing several racecourses, including Redcar, Thornaby, Catterick, Thirsk and owing to some accident of geography, York racecourse, although not the city of York itself. Our responsibility was the Knavesmire. For race duties, we were collected at our stations by a small personnel carrier and on this occasion, as we were heading for Redcar, I settled in my seat and found myself next to a young constable with a Scots accent. The number on his epaulette was 557. I was 575.

'Are you PC MacTavish?' I asked, thinking that he did have a look of me. We could indeed have been brothers ...

'Aye, Alastair,' and he extended his hand.

'Nick Rhea,' I said.

'Oh, you're PC Rhea!' he grinned. 'Inspector Pollock keeps calling me PC Rhea.'

'And he keeps calling me PC MacTavish,' I smiled.

We exchanged a few tales about Pollock's inability to tell us apart and then discovered that Pollock was the duty officer at the races. At that news, I reckoned we were in for a fun-laden day. Both MacTavish and I were allocated duties in the car park prior to the first race, and then, once the races started, we were to patrol in the paddock to keep the peace, deter drunks and watch out for pickpockets. Our briefings were given by a local sergeant who had no difficulty with our identities and we proceeded to our places of duty.

MacTavish, being new to the chore of racecourse car parking, was positioned on the entrance to our car park, which

offered the simplest of our duties. Inside there were me and
several other officers; we operated at the end of each row of
cars, filling in the gaps by a well-tested system of hand-signals.
We had to guide the cars in at a rapid rate and park them in
herring-bone fashion to facilitate a smooth and swift exit once
racing was over. MacTavish's job was simply to keep traffic
moving towards us and to help in preventing queues of cars
forming in the town on the approaches to the racecourse. But,
as the sergeant told us, 'Change places from time to time,
Rhea and MacTavish; Rhea, you give young MacTavish an
opportunity to do the herring-bone parking ... help him,
though, we don't want a cock-up.'

As MacTavish was waving his cars towards me, Inspector
Pollock passed by the youngster and I heard him ask,
'Everything in order, Rhea?'

'MacTavish, sir. I'm MacTavish. Rhea is over there,
parking the cars in rows.'

'Oh, yes, of course. Well, carry on, things are going
smoothly.'

Pollock then came to me and beamed. 'You're Rhea, aren't
you? MacTavish is on the entrance?'

'Yes, sir,' I smiled. 'You've got it right this time!'

'Yes, I can tell you apart now. Well, no problems? The
drivers are behaving? Obeying your signals?'

'Yes, sir, they're very experienced at this anyway, well,
most of them, that is. The newcomers can cause hold-ups, but
nothing serious. We're coping very well.'

Half an hour later, MacTavish and I were told to change our
places. I was on the entrance now, waving in the never-ending
stream of cars, and MacTavish was having his first real
attempt at herring-bone parking. He was coping quite well
when Inspector Pollock arrived at my point.

'Well done, MacTavish, you've learned this very well.'

'Rhea, sir. I'm PC Rhea. MacTavish is over there, parking
them in rows.'

He looked into the ranks of cars and shook his head. 'But I
thought Rhea was there ...'

'No, I'm here, sir, we've changed places. Sergeant's orders.'

'I ought to memorize your number, MacTavish ...'

'Rhea, sir.'

'So you are 575, Rhea.'

'Yes, sir, and MacTavish is 557.'

'That's not going to help, is it?' he grumbled, shaking his head. 'Well, I'd better go and see how MacTavish is getting along.'

By the time he returned for his third visit, we had swopped places again, and the confusion continued; it was even worse when we left the car parking to assume our duties in the paddock because in there we were free to roam anywhere and were not restricted to fixed points. But as the afternoon wore on, Inspector Pollock, being an office of superior intellect, found a compromise. He ceased to address us by name. He merely addressed us as 'Constable'.

And he did this thereafter. Thus I had lost my identity and the next time he saw me at Ashfordly, he asked, 'All correct, Constable?'

'Yes, sir, all's quiet.'

'That was a very good report you submitted about the careless driving incident,' he said. 'Seeing it was the first traffic accident you've had to deal with, you did a very good job. A very well-presented file.'

'That wasn't me, sir,' I smiled. 'That would be PC 557 MacTavish.'

'Aren't you MacTavish?'

'No, sir, I'm Rhea.'

Sadly, about a year later, PC MacTavish was asked to resign from the force because, under the terms of his probationary period, it was felt he would never make an efficient constable. I have often wondered if I had done something wrong or sloppily which might have been entered in his personal record by error and which might have soured his chances of being accepted as a constable in our force. But I never knew the reason for his early departure. Then, about two years later, a Scotsman stopped me in Strensford to ask directions to the harbourside.

'You're Jock MacTavish's lad, aren't you?' he suddenly asked as he looked into my face.

'No,' I said. 'My name is Rhea.'

'Are ye sure?' he grinned. 'You're not pulling my leg?'

'No,' I spoke in a strong Yorkshire accent. 'I'm the one with the Yorkshire accent.'

And he went away, shaking his head. 'I think you're kidding me, Alastair,' he said. 'Your dad said I'd find you here, at Strensford ...'

And to this day, I have no idea what became of Alastair MacKenzie MacTavish; if his father did not know where he was, then clearly there was a mystery about that ex-constable.

And, on reflection, I don't know the identity of the Scotsman who thought I was Alastair MacKenzie MacTavish, but for a long time after the departure of MacTavish, Inspector Pollock continued to call me 'Constable'.

★ ★ ★

Another occasion when Inspector Pollock became confused occurred when the Strensford Police football team won the Chief Constable's Cup and decided to hold their celebration party at the Aidensfield Arms. It was a Friday night and the team had booked a supper at the pub; George had applied for an extension of hours and promised to make a superb ham buffet, Arnold Merryweather's bus had been booked to convey the team to and from Strensford. The party promised to be a happy occasion.

Although the party was for team members and their spouses, the captain, Bob Oliver, did invite me to pop in. He also extended his invitation to the officers of Ashfordly Section. When the day of the party arrived I was dismayed to find that I was on duty, and so were Alf Ventress and Phil Bellamy, both of whom were keen football fans. But the fact that Phil was on duty that night was not necessarily a drawback – he said he might just pop in and so I said likewise. It would be churlish to avoid the party, we felt.

On that Friday night the heavens opened and the rain poured down. In my little van with its radio crackling in the comfort of the cab, I found nothing to do. I chugged around the moors and dales but found nothing to occupy me; everyone was sheltering from the storm but I had to patrol until midnight. I found myself getting utterly bored – and then I remembered the party at the inn. I had an invitation, but I was on duty – I decided I would pop in, as invited, but would not, of course, drink alcohol. I might be tempted to a soft drink or two, and some sandwiches. I convinced myself that I was not doing wrong because pub visits were part of my duty.

And so, at about 10.30, I parked my minivan at the rear of the pub under a carport and entered. Inside, the place was heaving with large off-duty policemen with their wives or girlfriends, and the regulars were there too. Among the packed crowd, I spotted the familiar shape of Claude Jeremiah Greengrass; his dog, Alfred, was dozing before the fire. And then I saw two police uniforms. At first, I thought the team was organizing some kind of joke, but I quickly realized that the uniformed men were Phil Bellamy and Alf Ventress. As I pushed through the crowd towards them, somebody thrust a pint of beer into my hand and disappeared before I could refuse it. Clutching the pint high above my head to avoid spillage, I managed to reach Alf and Phil.

'What are you two doing here? I thought you were on duty!'

'We are, we've sneaked over here for some supper,' grinned Bellamy.

Alf added, 'There's nobody about, the town's dead and we've got to close the police station for several hours a day now, part of the new plans, so me and Phil thought we'd drive out to this party. We were invited ...'

'What about Blaketon? Won't he wonder where you are?'

'He's on his long weekend off, he's gone away to the Lake District.'

'So who's in charge?'

'That dopey new inspector,' grinned Alf. 'Pollock. And he won't even know where to find the pub, let alone find us. Relax, Nick, we've left the car outside the back window with the radio on full volume; look, the window's open at the bottom, we'll hear our call sign if we're wanted for anything urgent.'

I could see the rear bar window was open a few inches, but the rain was not entering. And I could see the bodywork of their official car just outside. It meant that two official police vehicles were parked at the rear of the pub. There is a saying within police circles that a good policeman never gets wet, so we were helping to perpetuate that myth. We all knew, however, that if we got caught, we should be in serious trouble for being absent from our beats. That did not necessarily apply to me, of course, because I *was* on my beat and I could claim that I was performing a routine pub visit. Normally pub visits lasted two or three minutes, but this one would last all night!

The snag with radios in official vehicles was that every thirty minutes, at quarter to and quarter past the hour, we received a request from Control to state our current location. This meant that either Alf or Phil had to rush out of the pub every thirty minutes to respond to 'locations', as we termed the call. And in response to each call he gave a vague response such as 'Patrolling Ashfordly area' or 'Patrolling the A169 heading south' or 'Thackerston Moor, intend Elsinby and Crampton' or 'Rannockdale towards Whemmelby'. And so, in the minds of Control, the Ashfordly car appeared to be busily patrolling the district in pouring rain when in fact it was parked behind George's busy inn at Aidensfield. I could quite easily respond to each call by saying 'Patrolling Aidensfield and district.'

So, on that awful night, our cars remained at the inn while we talked football, had our suppers and socialized with the victorious Strensford team. The extension of hours had been granted until midnight and by half-past eleven the entire football team was well fed and watered. I must admit I had sipped from the pint which had been earlier thrust into my hands, but had restricted myself to that one alcoholic drink, although I did have a whopping big supper, several soft drinks and copious cups of coffee. Alf had sipped one pint of beer too and had then turned to orange juice, but Bellamy, not driving, had weakened – he had dealt with several pints and enough food to satiate a family of five.

And then I heard the distinctive sound of the Ashfordly car's official radio. It was Ventress's call sign, but it was not 'locations' – it was a duty call!

'Alf, Phil,' I said, 'you're wanted. Division's calling you up!'

Alf rushed out to the rear of the premises to respond. The

rain was cascading from the skies in a ferocious downpour and in the few seconds that it took to reach the car door he got drenched. He came back and said, 'That was Inspector Pollock, he asked for my location.'

'What did you say?' asked Phil, now very nervous.

'Well, he said he'd been checking our locations all night, driving to the places I'd mentioned hoping to rendezvous with us, and had missed us every time.'

'Oh God,' groaned Bellamy.

Ventress continued, 'He wants to know where the hell we've been! He wants an explanation – he said we could not have driven from Thackerston to Whemmelby without meeting him and if we'd been in Elsinby, he would have seen us ...'

'Where is now?' I asked.

'Aidensfield,' and the expression on Alf's face told us that his ruse had been rumbled. 'He's parked right outside the front door of this pub!'

It meant the three of us were trapped inside. Our police vehicles were at the back and there was no way out other than by the main entrance. We knew that Pollock would wait outside the pub. He was not as daft as we'd thought. We were in trouble.

'I'll check,' I said.

I rushed up to the first landing of George's staircase and peered through the window that overlooked the street; sure enough, Pollock's car was parked right opposite, its lights shining in the pouring rain. I could see him in the driver's seat, his white shirt collar gleaming through the damp window. We were in a dilemma now ... we had to find a logical reason why we had been here all this time, Alf and Phil had to find a reason to explain their mysterious non-tour of the district ... and the fact that the pub was full of off-duty policemen would make any excuse sound very feeble. But, as the Bible says, 'In the multitude of counsellers, there is safety.'

And there were lots of counsellers in the premises. I returned to the bar to impart my bad news to Alf and Phil, whereupon George approached me.

'Trouble, Nick?'

I explained our dilemma, urging George to be sure to close the premises on time, having regard to his extension of hours, of course, because Pollock was lingering outside. George said, 'This lot are leaving early, some have got to be on duty at 1 a.m., they were given three hours off for this. They'll be on their way before we have to shut.'

'That's not my real concern, George,' I said, 'We need a good reason for being here now, Alf, Phil and me.'

'Well, it's a foul night, Nick; nobody with any sense would be out in this weather, you'd never turn a dog out on a night like this!'

'That's it!' I had the answer. 'Dogs! We've been doing a humanitarian act, we've been out looking for Claude Jeremiah's dog. Claude told us the dog had got lost and he was worried, so we've been looking for it. How's that for a story? Claude will co-operate, surely?'

'It might cost you a few free pints for him, but you're not wet!' said George. 'Your uniforms are all dry!'

'Then we must go outside and stand in the downpour until we look wet ...' I said.

'And Alfred's as dry as a bone, Nick, he's been lying near that fire all night, he's as clean as a whistle ...'

'Then we'll have to wet him, we could bath him!' I said.

'Bath him? You're not using the hotel bathroom to bath that flea-ridden mongrel!' snapped George.

'You've an outbuilding and a bucket?' I asked.

'There's an old tin bath hanging inside that bottle shed round the back,' said George. 'You can use that if you want ...'

And so the urgent plot was hatched. In the few minutes that remained, and as the football team began to sing their final song, I asked Claude Jeremiah if we could borrow Alfred.

'Borrow my Alfred?' he frowned. 'He's very particular who he mixes with, is my Alfred.'

'He's been happy enough to eat all those bits of ham the policemen have given him,' I said. 'He likes these coppers, Claude. Besides, we could come to some arrangement about free drinks in here, for you, I mean.'

'Aye, well, if it's business you're talking ...'

And so, for the price of three free pints of beer every night for a week, Claude agreed to lend us Alfred and to say he had reported to us that Alfred had been lost in the storm. Silently, Alf Ventress, Phil Bellamy and I crept out of the rear door with Alfred on a lead, leaving the footballers to sing as loudly as possible so that Inspector Pollock would hear their dulcet tones. Outside, we allowed the rain to drench our uniforms and, from an outside tap, we filled an old bucket with water and threw it over the startled Alfred. We stood him in the old tin bath and swished gallons over the miserable dog until he looked as if he truly had been lost on the moors.

The poor dog was baffled by this treatment and did not like it one bit; he whined and struggled, he thrashed about which made us even wetter and shook himself so that each one of us was very wet very soon.

Eventually satisfied with his bedraggled appearance, we replaced the bath and bucket, climbed over the fence behind the pub into a ploughed field, got our boots, uniforms and the dog well and truly filthy with mud, and then trudged down a narrow path back into the village. I knew we could appear some distance from the pub's entrance.

The three of us, drenched and dirty, with Alfred resisting at the end of the lead, trudged through the street until we arrived at the pub door. There we could see the lights of Pollock's car, so we made towards them.

'Good evening, sir,' said Ventress, hauling Alfred to his side as he approached the car.

Pollock wound down the window and peered at the three of us. We must have been a sorry sight.

'What on earth's going on, Ventress? I've been touring the moors and dales looking for you, and for you, Rhea, and not a sign, not a sound ... not one of you answered my radio calls ... I came to the locations ...'

'We've been looking for this dog, sir, he's a valuable animal. He escaped from his owner and so, as a humanitarian act, we decided to look for him. Sorry we missed you, that would be when we got off the beaten track, into side roads, up farm lanes, along bridleways, looking for Alfred ... anyway, sir, we've found him.'

'It doesn't look like a very valuable animal to me,' said Pollock. 'In fact, it looks like a downright mongrel ... where's it from?'

'Aidensfield, sir,' I said. 'His owner is in the pub, we're just returning the dog to him.'

At that moment, the front door of the pub burst open and the Strensford Police football team poured forth.

Singing some bawdy song, they traipsed out of the pub and headed for their bus in the car park. Pollock watched them with a frown on his face.

'Isn't that Sergeant Jowett?' asked Pollock.

'Is it, sir?' said Alf Ventress. 'Your eyesight's better than mine ...'

'And PC Bateman ... and Campbell ... and Wood ...'

'Oh, they'll have been celebrating their win, sir, the Chief Constable's Cup,' I said. 'It had slipped my mind because of this dog ... the pub was granted an extension of hours, sir, for the party. You'll remember – the licence was approved by Ashfordly magistrates a month ago.'

'Yes, of course. I do remember. You know, it would have been nice to have joined them,' smiled Pollock. 'Especially on a night like this.'

'Yes, sir, but one's constabulary duty must be done,' said Alf with water dripping from the peak of his cap. And at that moment the door of the pub opened to reveal Claude Jeremiah Greengrass who stood in the light cast from within.

Playing his part like a hero, Claude shouted, 'Alfred, you old bugger, are you out there?'

Alfred whined and leapt towards his master; his sudden move meant that the wet lead slipped from Ventress's hands. The happy dog galloped across to Claude and leapt up to greet him. Alfred made a huge fuss and wagged his tail as Claude hugged him.

'A most touching scene,' smiled Inspector Pollock. 'Is that the owner?'

'Yes, sir,' I said.

'It's five minutes to midnight,' smiled Pollock, glancing at his watch. 'Five minutes to go before closing time, so I think that man ought to buy us all a drink, to thank you gentlemen for making such an effort to trace his dog.'

'A great idea!' beamed Ventress.

'I say, you,' said Pollock leaping from his car. 'You with the dog!'

Claude halted as the inspector galloped across the road.

'Me?' asked Claude, in amazement at the sight. 'What have I done now?'

'These men, officers of mine, I might add, have worked jolly hard tonight to find your dog, I believe.'

'Aye, they have. And I'm very grateful ...' Claude played his part very well. 'It's not often I'm grateful to the police but, well, on a night like this ...'

'There's just time for you to buy them all a drink, I can authorize them to take a drink on duty, being their senior officer, and there are just a few minutes left before the inn must close ... so might I suggest you buy us all a drink, to celebrate the recovery of your dog? And there are more of my men on the car park, just about to leave ... I might even persuade them to stay a few minutes more, just to celebrate the return of this dog ...'

'Me? Buy a load of coppers a drink?' blustered Claude. 'It's them that ought to be buying me a drink or two ...'

'Consider it an investment, Claude,' I said softly.

'Aye, well, if you put it like that. I'm just pleased I've got Alfred back safe and sound!' He meant every word of that final remark and so he trudged back into the pub with Alfred on his lead. Pollock brought in the bus-load of officers and we all had a drink, paid for by Claude Jeremiah Greengrass. George was astounded, I was worried but Alfred was happy. He shook himself all over Claude and then went to lie by the fire once more.

'Alfred, an odd name for a dog,' said Pollock.

'He's named after me,' said Alf Ventress. 'I rescued him as a puppy, somebody threw him in the river and I found him. I gave him to Mr Greengrass, who named the dog after me. So you see, sir, there was a sentimental reason for our work tonight.'

In the touching moments that followed, Claude leaned over to Ventress and said, 'You don't half talk a load of old mush!

That dog was never named after a copper ...'
    'It is now,' smiled Alf.

* * *

And so the police officers of Ashfordly, Strensford and district
settled down to await the impending changes. Most worried of
all was poor Sergeant Blaketon. He could see himself plodding
the beat in Strensford as a shift sergeant rather than being in
charge of his own section. This worry was compounded when
a sergeant and a constable from the Research and
Development department at force headquarters suddenly
arrived at Ashfordly police station.

    'We've come to measure your office, Oscar,' announced
Sergeant Higgins.

    'Measure it? What on earth for?' bellowed Blaketon.

    'We can't say, it's confidential,' said Higgins. 'It's all to do
with changes to the force structure, new divisions being
created, sections disappearing, that sort of thing.'

    And for the next half-hour, Sergeant Higgins and PC
Dawson measured Sergeant Blaketon's office and the enquiry
office with a long tape-measure. Dawson wrote down the
details in a shorthand notebook as the two men discussed
matters like offices for secretaries, toilets for women and
parking places for senior officers' cars.

    Poor Sergeant Blaketon just sat with a defeated look on his
face. He knew that Headquarters theorists worked in strange
ways but he did now think that Ashfordly police station was
earmarked for some future role of great importance. He also
got the impression that his humble office was being earmarked
for someone of high rank. It would be three weeks after that
visit, when I took my van into Headquarters garage for its
regular service, that I saw PC Alan Dawson.

    'I was on your patch the other week, Nick,' he said. 'With
Dan Higgins. We played a joke on Oscar Blaketon.'

    'A joke?' I asked. 'What kind of joke?'

    'Well, years ago, Blaketon dropped Higgins into the mire,
something pretty minor, it was. Blaketon should have
delivered a message from Higgins to the superintendent, but

he forgot. It was petty stuff, but as a result, Higgins got a bollocking from the superintendent.'

'So what was the joke?' I pressed.

'We were on our way to Scarborough police station,' smiled Alan Dawson. 'We just dropped into Ashfordly police station and measured it. Measuring someone's office always gets the incumbent worried – we told him it was confidential, something to do with impending changes in the Force structure. He'll worry about that for months now.'

'The Serious Rumour Squad in action?' I smiled.

'Some rumours have a habit of becoming fact,' he said, leaving me to ponder *that* statement. So was something important really going to happen at Ashfordly and Aidensfield? Or was it just a rumour? I could only wait and see.